LITTLE WILD FLOWER

Book One

WRITTEN BY
Samantha Jillian Bayarr

Bernice Florence
1019 Charles St.
Defiance, OH 43512

LivingstonHallPublishers.com
Look for Livingston Hall Publishers on Face Book

Library of Congress Cataloging-in-Publication Data

Samantha Jillian Bayarr
    Little Wild Flower
        ISBN 1453602968
151 p.   TXU001026312   2002-01-09

Also by Samantha Jillian Bayarr

LITTLE WILD FLOWER

Book One

WRITTEN BY
Samantha Jillian Bayarr

TABLE OF CONTENTS

LITTLE WILD FLOWER

Book Two

Sneak Peek

PROLOGUE

Jane Abigail Reeves was in denial. At least that's how her older sister Nadine described her. Raised as a city girl in a dysfunctional, middle-class family, Jane found it impossible to recognize what normal was anymore. In 1977, her father purchased a farm in the heart of a rural Amish community in Indiana when Jane was only fifteen. Jane and her siblings had not been brought up Plain, but their father had used the move as a means to start a new life. He made it out to be a grand adventure for his family to live off the land, "Like the Amish do," he had said so many years ago.

Jane knew the real reason her father wanted to move the family away from the city. Part was out of a need to save her mother from ridicule and judgment from unforgiving friends and family who couldn't see past her condition or accept her recovery from alcoholism. The other part, she knew, was her father's way of giving in to her mother's unquenchable desire to run from her past mistakes with the hope of putting them behind her.

For nearly three months, her mother had spent time attending counseling programs, which included a six-week stay in an alcohol rehabilitation clinic, until finally, one unforgettable day; she had managed to come home to her family. Soon after her mother returned home from the clinic, Jack Reeves made an announcement he would move his newly pregnant wife, Anna Mae, and their seven children, including Jane, from a large city in Michigan. The move to the Amish community was almost unbearable for Jane at the time. She didn't believe living out in the country, with horse-driven buggies, was something she felt she could ever accept.

In her stubbornness, Jane sat in her strange, new bedroom full of anger and resentment for the first two months after the move. She missed nearly her entire first summer at the new farmhouse, and even missed out on making friends the way her siblings had. Her older sister, Nadine, had tried on several occasions to coax her out of her room. She, too, wanted to have something better to do than hang around the warm house all summer, but Jane was too determined to brood. She'd been forced to leave her friends and modern conveniences back at her childhood home, all for the sake of a mother whom she wasn't immediately open to forgiving at the time.

The Reeves family adapted quickly to their new environment, save Jane, who rebelled against everything from having to use an outhouse, to staring at a blank television in a house with no electricity. The changes, however, that her family went through became easier, and had also brought about their new way of life as they settled into their new farmhouse in the Amish community.

If the truth be told, Jane in fact loved the openness of the country, and admired the Plain lifestyle of the Amish folk that surrounded their farm. And though she initially rebelled, she knew her mother's plans for recovery depended on a simpler way of life. After all, Jane's entire life up until about six months prior to the move had been full of cruel treatment that she had suffered at the hands of her then-alcoholic mother. Prompted by her childhood friend, Bradley, whom she dearly missed, Jane built up enough courage to get her mother the help she needed. Directly after the move, she had some regrets over the decision, but when she saw how much it meant to her mother and the rest of her family, she felt guilty for being so selfish.

In spite of all that had happened, Jane and her mother became very close during that unsure period in their lives. While her thoughts remained with those early days in their farmhouse, a warm peace settled in Jane's heart.

Oh, how happy I was then. In spite of all my protestin' and anger about movin' here and missin' my friends back home, I've loved it from the very beginning. As a matter of fact, from the very first day I sat on the porch swing of our new house...

ONE
A TIME TO GROW

Little Rachel Zook was the first of our new neighbors to make her acquaintance with me. The Zook's best milking cow, Ida, had gotten loose one early autumn day, finding its way to the next farm over—ours. I was too determined to brood to pay her any mind, or to be bothered by what was going on around me. And in my quest to shut out the world, an entire herd of cows might have been able to walk right by me unnoticed. We'd been here for over two months already, but this was the first time I'd been outside of the house.

I sprawled lazily across the wooden porch swing, daydreaming of how much better my life would be if I'd never suggested to my father that my mother needed a change of scenery. Though moving to an Amish community was not what I had in mind, I had to admit my mother had seemed much happier since the move. I, on the other hand, was miserably lonely without my friends to see me through.

I'd gotten a few letters from friends I knew from school, but since I never wrote them back, they gave up. I didn't see any point in keeping in touch by mail, since I knew I'd never have another conversation with them. With no phone, I felt cut off from everyone, and that was how it would stay.

I pushed the swing lazily with one foot, while the rhythmic squeaking of the old, rusty chain that suspended the swing had nearly lulled me to sleep. I let one arm dangle across the slats of the porch; the other neatly tucked under my head for comfort. Mindlessly twisting my long, blonde hair between my fingers, I gave in to thoughts of self-pity.

Startled by movement from across the long-stretched yard, I squinted my blue eyes against the afternoon sun. Taking in a deep breath, I could almost taste the ripe apples from the small orchard that stood between the two properties. When I finally looked in the direction of the commotion, I spotted a young girl working her way around the unkempt fence that established the property line separating us from our neighbors. I came to a sudden halt from my gentle swinging and sat upright to get a better look at the curly-haired tot as she struggled with the broken, whitewashed fence. Her clothing was just as my father had described to me just weeks before our move. A sudden shift of the wind tipped her bonnet off her head to reveal dark, blonde curls. Her apron fluttered around in the breeze, causing her agitation as she tried to free the hem of her long dress from the fence. I held a hand over my mouth to cover up my laughter. As she walked bashfully toward me, I straightened up, burying my amusement over her struggle with the fence. My efforts were in vain, however, for she introduced herself with downcast eyes.

"I'm Rachel Zook, and our milking cow got loose."

She spoke with the same German accent I'd remembered from the man who talked with my parents regarding the sale of our farm. It had seemed like a lifetime before, but had only been a few weeks ago that I'd sat at the top of the stairs and watched my father converse with the strange, bearded man. His wife had spent many a day with my mother, sharing Amish recipes and folklore. While I had enjoyed the wonderful food they prepared together, I had carefully avoided contact with all of the neighbors—up until now.

Rachel adjusted her bonnet to sit squarely on her head, and then continued to speak.

"Could ya help me look for the cow? I think it came over this way, *jah*?"

Her eyes looked up slightly, enough for me to see a slight hint of mischief in them.

Though I was immediately intrigued by this small stranger, I pursed my lips and sighed heavily, determined that no one would interrupt my right to sit on the porch swing and brood.

"I saw a cow go that way." I lied. But I pointed in the direction of the field behind our farm hoping she would go away.

"Will ya show me, please?" the little girl begged.

"Can't ya ask somebody else?" I'm only out here because my mother said I was beginning to resemble a vampire in need of fresh air.

"I'm sorry. I didn't mean to bother ya, but you're the only one out here."

She pushed out her lower lip as she cast her eyes toward the ground.

"Now you're actin' just like my little sisters. I'll help ya look for the cow—as long as ya quit lookin' at me like that."

She flashed me a brief smile. "Are you Lucy's sister?"

"Yep, that's what they tell me. I'm Jane. And I'm guessin' that if ya know my sister, then ya must be around her age."

I stepped off the porch and stuffed my hands into the back pockets of my cut-off jeans, intending to help her look for the cow.

"I'm five years and eleven months to be exact. I'll be going to the schoolhouse in September, Miss Jane."

"Why in the world did ya call me 'Miss'? I already told ya my name is Jane—just Jane."

"I must say it that way because my papa says it's *gut* and proper-like."

"I hope ya don't expect me to call ya Miss Rachel."

She shook her head as I was talking.

"You would only call me "Miss" if I was older than you; that's what my papa says."

I didn't completely understand, but I let the matter drop—mostly because I didn't really care.

"My father said we're gonna have to go to your little school house because our old school is too far away. In another state—to be exact," I mocked her. "B'sides, he don't want us goin' to public school no more. 'Says it's not a good place for us to learn our values."

"So you'll be converting?" she asked.

I scrunched up my face. "Converting to what?"

"The Amish ways," she said gently.

"No way! We're just goin' to school with ya. I don't think this Amish stuff is cool at all—only my dad—I mean my *papa* does."

She looked at me only for a moment, but stood politely quiet next to me.

"I'd be willin' to bet the school bus couldn't even find us way out here in "no-wheres-ville," I said under my breath.

"What did ya say, Miss Jane?"

"Never mind," I said. "I wasn't really talkin' to you. And quit lookin' at me like that, you're botherin' me."

She quietly apologized as we stepped out along the path that was surrounded by wild flowers so we could look for the stray cow. I searched as far as the horizon in every direction pretending to look for the cow, but really I was looking for any sign of a town or civilization of any kind. All I could see were a few homes, lots of trees, and plenty of animals.

Discouragement settled in the deep frown that had recently come to be a permanent expression on my face.

"Ya don't seem like ya want to live here," Rachel said, breaking the sudden, awkward silence.

My frown grew deeper. "I never asked to live here if that's what ya mean. I had to leave my best friends and a big school back home. I don't feel like I belong here."

She held out her arms in a wide circle and flashed me a smile.

"None of this makes me unhappy. It's wonderful *gut* to live here if ya can learn to love it."

"I'm not so sure I could ever be happy here. I miss my friends—and TV—and havin' a bathroom inside the house."

"What's wrong with the outhouse in the yard?" Rachel asked.

"It just isn't the same—trust me. Besides, it's 1977 not 1877. People don't need to use outhouses anymore since plumbing was invented. For cryin' out loud—I don't know why I'm even bothering to tell ya this stuff."

"My papa says God gave me *gut* ears so I could be a *gut* listener," she said.

I forced a smile when she looked at me, and I could almost see the honesty in her big, brown eyes. We walked a little further until we reached the edge of the pasture from where the cow escaped.

"What's wrong?" Rachel suddenly asked. "Are ya sick, Miss Jane?"

"No. Why?"

"Why are ya holding your hand over your nose?"

"I don't like the way it smells here," I said, coughing lightly.

She cupped her hand around her mouth and leaned in close as if to whisper in my ear.

I leaned in a little as though I was interested in her secret. "You smell the cows. They don't use the outhouse."

I chuckled a little. "Maybe they should."

"You will get used to it. Papa calls it good fresh country air, and says there's no point in complaining about things when there's nothing you can do about it."

"Well, I say you talk too much!"

She stopped along the path to pick a few of the different flowers that grew wild in the tall grass.

I considered walking away from her, but I wasn't ready to return to my solitude on the porch swing just yet. "We've got a big family like all the families around here. My father says that's why we'll have no trouble fitting in.

We've got two boys and five girls so far. My mother's gonna have another one after Christmas."

I had no idea why I was suddenly breaking my own rule of silence with this child, but it almost seemed a relief to speak out.

"I have one older sister named Rebekah," she said. "She likes your brother, Mitchell."

I had watched Rebekah with my older brother from my bedroom window, and the two seemed inseparable. She was all he talked about at the dinner table every night, and I was getting tired of hearing how happy he was when I was so miserable.

"I've got two older brothers named Samuel and Elijah, and *Mam's* going to have twins soon."

"Is *Mam* what ya call your mother?"

"*Jah,*" she said. "My two cousins, Luke and Daniel, live with us since my Uncle Abner and Aunt Esther died."

"Wow, they didn't die in the house did they?"

The very subject of death made me feel uneasy, but the thought of living in a house that once belonged to dead people made my stomach suddenly turn. Mitchell had always teased me about there being ghosts in the basement of our old house, and I suppose I'd developed a fear of the unknown because of it.

She shook her head casually, and ignored my question as she continued to talk of her family.

"My brother Elijah is about your age. Do ya want to meet him?" she asked, appearing to be sizing me up.

"Yeah. Sure. I'll meet him some time." Truth was; I didn't want to meet anyone.

"He's in the field with my papa. We can go out there to look for Ida and you can meet Elijah at the same time. Maybe if you make a friend you won't miss the one's you can't see anymore."

She grabbed my hand and pulled me in the direction of the field. I didn't like her suggestion because I had no intention of replacing my friends, so I gently pulled away from her.

"Maybe later." Man, she's a pushy little thing.

She seemed to get the message and let the matter drop.

"Please tell me more about your family," she begged, as we walked side-by-side along the path.

"Okay. You already know my brother Mitchell. He's eighteen and a half. Then there's Nadine, who's almost seventeen, and I'm almost sixteen. When I was six, my mother had my sister, Rachel who's nine; then Cameron, my brother came along. He's seven. Then there's Lucy; she's almost six."

"I'm already *gut* friends with Lucy. We're going to sit together in school," she said.

"Ya already told me you're friends with Lucy. Anyway; after Lucy is Molly, she's the youngest at three, but only until the new baby is born. My parents are hopin' they'll have another boy, but I'd rather have all sisters."

I stopped talking and rolled my eyes when I realized that the child had lost interest in what I'd been saying. She led me along the trail, calling out for Ida, until we reached the back of her farm. Their farm mirrored ours, with two homes and an out-house next to the barn. Tall grasses provided segue to the growing fields that furnished a means of capital for the Amish farmers.

We followed the trail through the tall grass that led to a field that seemed to stretch out over several acres. A few feet in front of me, a handsome, teen-aged boy stopped working alongside a large man, bailing hay. They both had on short-sleeved, white shirts and brown trousers with suspenders, and wide-brimmed hats. I could see wisps of dark blonde hair falling out along the boy's slightly tanned face while he stared as we approached them. I recognized the older man as Abraham Zook, the man who'd sold our farm to my family. He wore a long beard with no mustache, in the traditional Amish style.

Upon our abrupt appearance, one of the brown and white horses reared slightly, jostling the primitive farm equipment to which it was attached. The wide, flat wagon behind it was hooked to a separate team of horses. It was full of round hay bales stacked high, which I thought closely resembled giant Shredded Wheat Biscuits. They didn't look at all like the square bails of straw my father had bought in town for our barn.

"*Gut* afternoon, Miss."

Mr. Zook tipped his hat slightly toward me.

I clasped my hands behind me, nodding nervously. I hated formal introductions, and momentarily felt anger rise up in me toward Rachel for luring me here.

"What are you two girls doing out in the fields on such a hot day?" he asked Rachel as he fanned his face with his hat.

"Elijah, this is Jane," she said, ignoring her father's question. "She's Lucy's older sister, and she's helping me look for Ida. She got loose again. I thought I saw her go over to their house, but maybe I was wrong."

She giggled as her attention darted back and forth between Elijah and me.

"That will be enough of the teasing for now, Rachel," Abraham said.

"Yes, Papa," she said with downcast eyes.

She just had to draw attention to me, didn't she? Is it too late to run off? Elijah might think I'm a baby if I run, so I'll stay put. "Nice to meet you."

Elijah tipped his hat toward me, causing my cheeks to flush. I nodded, then, turned my face away from Elijah's, pretending as though I were looking for a cow that I'd never seen before. I struggled with my thoughts, keeping my back to him so he wouldn't see the redness that I could feel sweeping over my face. I wasn't certain what it was that embarrassed me so when Elijah looked at me. Maybe it was because I felt an immediate attraction toward him because he was much different from any of the boys at the public school I had attended.

Maybe Rachel made a mistake about our ages. Elijah looks older than me. But if he's Nadine's age, oh, I'll be so bummed out. He's such a fox.

My thoughts surprised me. I'd never been in competition with Nadine and I wasn't about to start now. How could I be jealous when Elijah hadn't even shown any real interest in me? After all, we just met. I pushed the thought from my mind as best I could and began to walk away from the three of them because I was certain my hot face had turned a shade of red that would surely reveal my intimate thoughts. I wondered how it was that I hadn't seen this boy before now, and chided myself for wasting the entire summer in my room.

If I'd known I had such a cute neighbor, I might have left the house long before now.

"It was a pleasure meeting you, Jane," Mr. Zook said before I walked out of earshot.

"Me too," I said over my shoulder.

My voice cracked, exposing the awkwardness I felt over meeting Elijah. I held up a hand, turning only my shoulder behind me to wave, as I continued to walk away.

"Jane, please wait for me," Rachel called after me, running to catch up.

After a few minutes of walking together in silence, Rachel spoke up again.

"Elijah was staring at you for sure and for certain!"

Her comment took me by surprise but I tried not to let it show. I pulled a tall piece of grass from the field and began twisting it around my fingers, suddenly realizing I'd somehow lost the flowers that I'd picked only a few minutes earlier.

"How old is he anyway?" I asked, shrugging as though I didn't really care what the answer was.

"He's almost seventeen. Nearly ready to marry soon, Papa says."

I raised an eyebrow at her, but didn't comment. Normally, I would have never believed such an answer, except for the fact that my father had sat the whole family down before our move to explain what our new neighbors would be like.

Growing up in a big city made it next to impossible to believe that people actually still drove horse-driven buggies instead of a car. It all seemed so backward to us as he explained it. Still, we sat with eyes wide, as my father prepared us for the type of language we would hear and the things we would see once our move was official. I'd forgotten that my father had tried hard to convince us that a lot of the Amish were married by the time they reached eighteen. None of it seemed real at the time my father explained it, but Rachel's statement had made it a reality for me. I felt a little unnerved, not knowing what bothered me more at the moment; the fact that Elijah was indeed the same age as Nadine, or that he might be looking for a girl to marry. I pushed the silly thoughts aside for the time being so I could concentrate on helping Rachel look for the cow. After all, I certainly had nothing better to do, and this little girl had somehow captured my curiosity. It's funny how quickly something so simple can change things and put them in perspective, for I suddenly realized that looking for a cow was the most excitement I'd had in months.

TWO
A TIME TO LEARN

On September fifth, school was officially open. In spite of my father's many talks, I wasn't truly prepared for what I saw as I entered the one-room schoolhouse. Neither was Nadine.

We walked into the entrance to an area lined with bookshelves on one side; wooden pegs for coats on the other side. Above the pegs was a shelf already filled with round metal pails I suspected contained food; the smell of fried chicken mixed with rain-soaked suede coats, hung in the air. Nadine and I stood at the doorway and stared for some time. I wanted to leave, but where would I go for an entire day?

I tugged on Nadine's arm. "We aren't gonna stay here for real, are we?"

Nadine narrowed her eyes and gritted her teeth. "You heard what your father said. We have to stay here all day—every day."

"He's yer dad too, Nadine. You need to stop disowning mom and dad whenever yer mad. Ya make yerself sound so stupid when ya do that."

My father expected us to be in school all day, and in school we would be whether we wanted to or not.

When we finally mustered up the nerve to step inside, the other kids scattered about as though being there was second-nature to them. Nadine and I, on the other hand, looked as out of place as a couple of hippies in an uptown office.

I looked around trying to make some sense of it, but it all seemed so primitive. A homemade sign painted in black lettering hung above the door that read "Coat Room"; as if we didn't already know. Rebekah Zook, the schoolteacher and my brother, Mitchell's girlfriend, greeted us cheerfully as we entered the over-sized schoolroom full of children of all ages. Several rows of long tables filled the room; wooden chairs pushed neatly beneath them. On top of the tables sat a McGuffey Reader for each place setting in the first three rows. The older children were instructed to sit in the back two rows.

In the front of the room, a chalkboard covered the entire wall. The east and west walls consisted of tall windows, reaching nearly from floor to ceiling. Along the back wall, a length of rope with clothes pins for the hanging of wet coats was fashioned under a row of several worn maps that were attached with straight pins. After attending such a large high school, I suddenly realized it was going to take a lot of adjusting to get used to learning in such a small environment.

Is Elijah coming?" Nadine asked Rebekah.

I cringed.

Why can't that girl learn to keep her big mouth shut?

Nadine and I had secretly watched Elijah from the fence line for the previous two weeks. I disliked the idea of having Nadine tag along on such an important adventure, but I knew she would tattle on me if I refused to let her go. Nadine was just as interested in him as I was, but I was certain I had an advantage over Nadine to win Elijah's heart since I'd recently made his acquaintance and she had not.

"The older boys don't come back to school 'til harvesting season is all finished up, but Elijah won't be here at all since he's too old. The boys don't usually come to learn past eighth grade, and most times, the girls don't come either if they're needed at home."

I nudged Nadine. "So tell me again why I didn't stay home?"

"I ain't goin' over this again, Jane. Ya know we ain't allowed to stay home. Dad don't care that we're past the eighth grade. We *have* to go to school, and that's the end of it."

"Ya don't gotta snap at me. I didn't make the rules."

"Besides," Nadine said. "I thought I'd come and see what it was all about. I think it would be fun to see what the Amish are learnin'."

Nadine sounded nervous. She was trying too hard to cover up her embarrassment over being at the school, and I wasn't buying the act she was putting forth for Rebekah's sake. The only thing I didn't understand was why Rebekah even registered us if we were too old to attend. Other than our father's stern persistence over continuing our education, the only thing we might learn here would be the values that he insisted upon. Right now, though, I was in total envy of my brother for finishing at the public school back home.

Rebekah cleared her throat. "Deborah Yoder is here, but Lydia stays home to help with the harvesting of their orchard. Deborah is trying for her teacher's certificate."

"She's gonna teach?"

Nadine was practically screeching.

Deborah and Nadine had become friends, but her tone made me wonder if this new bit of information would change all that. I knew Nadine's competitive nature all too well, and she was never keen on the idea of someone being one-up on her.

"Maybe you could teach too, Nadine," Rebekah offered. "Because you went to public school, you may be ahead of Deborah. And if I am to marry your brother, I won't have any need for my teaching certificate. The Elders will need someone to fill the position."

The look of satisfaction on Nadine's face told me she was eager to learn more about teaching, though I wanted no part of it. As far as Lydia was concerned, we'd met her briefly a few months back. She, too, had been interested in my brother, Mitchell, but Rebekah had won his heart. Mitchell and Molly were the only kids in my family not in attendance at the one-room schoolhouse, since Mitchell had graduated and Molly was only three.

As I gazed about the room, I noticed that all the female students were wearing the traditional long skirts or dresses and aprons with white *kapps* on their heads. The boys had on trousers with suspenders, collared shirts, and wide-brim straw hats—much like the one I'd noticed Elijah wearing every day in the fields.

I nudged Nadine and pointed slightly, drawing her attention to the others. She ignored me. It felt awkward that she and I were the only girls in trousers—even Rachel and Lucy had worn their summer dresses. I wondered if we were expected to wear dresses to school, even though Rebekah hadn't mentioned it to our mother when she put our names in her school roster. After a heavy sigh, I decided it best to push the thought from my head, knowing there was nothing to be done about it until later.

Rebekah began to write upon the black board, so Nadine and I took a seat with the older girls.

"Today," she began. "Is Monday, September fifth, nineteen hundred, seventy-seven; the year of our Lord."

It's 1977; the year of disco. Man, I miss listening to my record player.

Rebekah was still speaking, but I just couldn't concentrate.

"I have written it out for the younger children. I would like everyone to write their name and the date at the top of a piece of paper and write down what they did over the summer. We'll be sharing at the end of the school day."

Oh great. I knew it was a waste of time to come here. The last thing I wanna do is write an assignment for babies.

Everything I started to write had to be erased. I wasn't about to share with a bunch of strangers that we moved here after my mother sobered up in a clinic; or that I spent most of my summer crying in my strange, new room because I missed my friends back home. My father had been right about one thing, we had started all over in this strange place, and there was no reason to reveal our secret past to any of them. Since there wasn't anything I could write that would be of any interest—except the secret that Nadine and I shared about spying on Elijah, I wrote about Ida. I wrote about the dumb cow, and everyone loved it!

ଓଓଷ

When school was dismissed, I endured the long walk home. I skipped ahead of Daniel Zook and my brother, Cameron, who had tried several times to toss their ball over my head. All the kids in my family had already made friends—except me, and I really wasn't interested in making any in this boring place.

Upon entering the long, dirt drive that led to the house, I noticed the plumbing truck, which was once again parked right in front of the house, drawing a lot of attention among the neighbors.

Miller's Plumbing had worked for two straight weeks putting modern plumbing throughout the house, and had even turned a storage closet upstairs into a bathroom. Abraham Zook had been over once or twice to voice his protest in the beginning, but my father cordially reminded him that we weren't Amish, and we could no longer tolerate hauling the water in from the well just to bathe. I was happy because I wasn't looking forward to having to run to the outhouse in the middle of the night in the dead of winter. Yes, a bathtub and toilet suited me just fine, since it was something I'd grown up having.

Still, seeing the truck made me realize my family wasn't doing a very good job of trying to fit in with the community. I also feared we would lose the Zook's friendship, which would destroy any chance I had at getting Elijah's attention. I figured Mr. Zook's protesting over the plumbing was due to his attachment to the house since it had belonged to his brother, Abner, up until he died. But every time I saw Mr. Zook, he was every bit as pleasant as always. It was a good thing too, because I'd overheard my father tell my mother he had plans to have the county hook up electricity.

When I entered the door to the main house, my mother and Naomi Zook looked up at me from their sewing.

"There's lemonade out on the porch if you're thirsty," my mother said as I passed through the room.

"Don't have time. I'm lookin' for Mitchell," I said over my shoulder.

What I really meant was that I didn't want to get caught up in adult talk—especially not the Amish folklore I'd overheard too many times already. I'd convinced myself the stories bored me, though I'd found myself listening intently on a few occasions when the two of them didn't know I was lurking about the house.

"We made fresh cookies." Naomi's voice was faint by the time I reached the kitchen.

I ignored them, and quickly poured a glass of lemonade before running out through the kitchen door to the *Dawdi Haus* out back. A quick holler let me know Mitchell wasn't there so I ran out to the main field, which is where I'd been able to find him in recent days. He had offered to work the land for a small monthly wage so my father could continue to work in town until all the money was raised for our first year of operating the farm. In addition to his wage, my parents let him live in the *Dawdi Haus*. My father explained that the extra house is normally used for the grandparents to reside in when one of the sons takes over the farm after he marries. My parents said they would rather live in the main house until each of us kids was old enough to be out on our own, and Mitchell seemed fine with that arrangement because it meant he could have his own place.

My mother had her own contribution to the farm, with Naomi and a few other women to teach her how to use the wood cook stove. My father's stomach was always pleased with my mother's learning, and so was Mitchell's after a hard day in the fields. She was also learning to can vegetables and fruits for winter storage. My father and Mitchell had already used the smoke house to cure some ham from the pig that the Zook's had given us as a welcome gift.

My father was also pleased with the way my younger siblings had begun to fashion their language after our neighbors—I was still a little unsure about the idea of calling my parents *Mam* and *Papa,* but it was something I was beginning to get used to hearing. My parents even encouraged Mitchell to begin courting Rebekah Zook just before school began. In the eyes of the community, at eighteen, she was almost too old to be courting, but my brother had taken a shine to her and was quite pleased that Abraham had given his consent for the two to court "proper-like."

Normally, marriage to outsiders was strictly forbidden, but my father informed us that the Zook's and the surrounding community had changed a few years back by relaxing most of the Old Order customs. None of us really understood everything about it, but I knew it meant their rules had changed, allowing Mitchell and Rebekah the opportunity to marry, as long as he took on most of her traditional ways and honored her beliefs. Mitchell was so smitten with the schoolteacher that he was determined to become a farmer for her sake.

After stepping carefully over the clumps of earth that had been turned over, I reached Mitchell in the middle of the field with the lemonade I'd grabbed from the screened porch. He looked more pleased to see the glass of lemonade in my hand than he was to hear how my first day at the schoolhouse had gone.

"Ya brought that for me, right?"

I didn't answer.

Mitchell wiped the sweat from his brow with a red bandanna that he pulled from the back pocket of his dusty trousers. Thick, wet strands of his dark hair stuck to his sunburned forehead. Sweat continued to drip from his hair onto his face, so he tied the bandanna around his head. He hopped down from the tractor and punched my arm playfully.

"I see ya brought me some lemonade."

He grabbed the lemonade from me and gulped it down, then, handed the glass back to me.

"I drank outta that glass," I teased. "I back-washed in it."

"Ya did not, shorty, because if ya did, I'd have to rub yer face in the dirt."

"I'm not short," I barked. "Ya just grew more than I did, that's all."

"Yeah, and I got bigger muscles than you, too," he said as he flexed his biceps.

He relaxed his hand, then, grimaced, holding his palms open, revealing red and blistered hands.

"I guess yer not so tough after all." I held a hand over my mouth to cover my grin.

"Did ya come out here for a reason, or did ya just come out here to make fun of me?"

"Don'tcha even wanna hear 'bout my day at the little school house?" I begged. "By the way, if ya marry Miss Rebekah, you're gonna have to give up this modern tractor and drag a horse through them fields."

"Don't tease me. And don't ya go worryin' 'bout my business. Abraham ain't mad at Papa anymore for puttin' plumbin' in the house and all. He got over it after the first week of the Miller's truck bein' in the driveway. So he ain't gonna bother me none 'bout havin' a tractor. B'sides, ya need to start watchin' what ya say. The Amish boys like to tease a fella if they find out he's courtin'.'"

"Listen to yourself. You're really becoming one of them, aren't you?" I asked, suppressing laughter.

He pursed his lips and punched me in the arm again.

"Ouch, that hurt."

"Ooh, don't be such a baby. So, ya gonna tell me how yer day went? I'll bet it would have been more fun if Elijah had been there today instead of in them fields over thar with his papa."

"If I can't tease you, then ya can't tease me either. And don't say stuff like that, somebody might hear ya. Then I'll get in trouble for thinkin' on boys when I ain't supposed to yet. I'll make ya a deal—if you'll be keepin' my secret, I'll be keepin' yers."

I pushed out my lower lip in an effort to stifle his laughter toward my seemingly hopeless situation.

"Ya don't gotta beg. Hang in there," he said as he punched my arm again. "Maybe Papa will reconsider his decision next month when ya turn sixteen. Who knows, maybe ya could start comin' to Sunday Night Singin's if yer lucky," he added.

"What in the world is a Sunday Night Singin'?"

"Well if ya hadn't spent the first few months in yer room after we moved here, poutin' like a spoiled child, you would know more 'bout what goes on around here," he said, nodding his head and raising his eyebrow as though he had information that was privy to him alone.

"Wait just a minute," I interrupted. "The only reason I stayed in my room is 'cause our parents moved me away b'fore Bradley came to visit his grandma for the summer. I was just mad because I missed out on seein' him this year. After bein' somebody's best friend for so many years, it ain't easy givin' him up, ya know."

"Ya don't gotta convince me. I know ya miss Bradley, but ya gotta move on with yer life. Ya should've gotten his new address if ya wanted to stay in touch with him. It ain't easy, but ya gotta learn to live with the mistake ya made in not gettin' his address last year," he said.

"It ain't my fault. I didn't know we were gonna move, and he was the best friend I'd ever had, besides Penelope. And we both know I'll never see her again either since she got put in a foster home last year. That's two best friends gone in one year, and I just can't take any crap from you about it."

"C'mon, let's not argue. Before ya get yer feathers ruffled over somethin' ya ain't got any control over, put your energy into what friends ya can get now, and make sure ya don't lose any more," he said as he gave me an affectionate squeeze.

"I'm sorry. I didn't mean to get off track. Weren't ya gonna give me the skinny on Sunday Singin's?"

He smiled at me, letting me know that we were settled in our disagreement, then, continued with his explanation.

"Singin's are what ya do when you're courtin' an Amish girl. Usually it's at someone's barn and only the youth in the area are allowed—especially if you're courtin' someone. We sing songs and play games. It really is a lot of fun. Rebekah and I have gone to a few, but we don't let on to any of the fellas that we're courtin' one another. If we had, we'd have gotten teased somethin' awful. For some reason or another, Amish boys like to tease ya when they find out you're courtin' someone."

"Would ya talk to Dad—*Papa* for me, Mitchell?"

"Don't beg."

"But ya don't understand. If I can just get Elijah to notice me, then maybe I'll have a chance to go to one of them Singin's with him," I said.

"Oh, he's already noticed ya plenty. 'Says he likes yer long blonde hair." He flicked a wavy spiral from my shoulder and I pushed at his arm.

"Is that what he said?"

Mitchell just stood there, staring at me like I hadn't said a word to him.

I stomped my feet playfully. "Tell me," I demanded.

"Hold on a minute. You're so giddy; the whole county is gonna mistake your jumpin' around for an earthquake."

The excitement left me as soon as he made his comment.

"That's not funny."

"Well I had to say somethin' to get your attention. Papa said ya had to be seventeen to have a beau, and unless he changes his mind, ya ought to hold your horses a bit. A year could be a long wait if you're gonna be this excited about it now. If Elijah's really interested, he'll wait on ya. And ya can be sure he'll be proper around ya, so ya better start thinkin' properly 'bout him, or you'll lose him to another girl," he warned me.

Listening to Mitchell talk this way made it hard to believe that only a few short years ago I had felt nothing short of hatred for him because of his mean disposition. I had, in fact, despised my entire family because none of them ever cared to be kind to one another, much less to help another member with a problem. Oh, occasionally, Nadine and I would put our heads together, but it usually meant trouble for the both of us. Now Mitchell was grown up and every bit of what a big brother ought to be. He no longer carried the hatred in his heart that made him ugly. In fact, he'd grown to be quite handsome with the added feature of a kinder disposition, and Rebekah was right to have chosen him.

I walked away from Mitchell with the empty glass in my hand, forgetting that I wanted to tell him what a great teacher *his* Rebekah had been. The only thing on my mind was how to create an opportunity to talk to Elijah. I knew it wouldn't be easy with his papa by his side in the field all day. I even worried that I might need to employ some of the workings of the "old Jane" in order to come up with a plan that would work.

Unable to think of anything that wasn't devious, I left the glass on the back porch and walked slowly toward the Zook farm feeling quite discouraged. Rachel was on the front porch with Lucy, shelling peas with an older girl I thought I recognized from school.

"Hello, Jane. This is my cousin Hannah. She lives across the road."

Rachel pointed to a grey farmhouse set back off the road. It was tough to see through the trees that lined the road in front of the property. In fact, I hadn't even realized there was a farm there until she pointed it out, as I hadn't yet explored much of my new surroundings.

"She's the same age as you," Rachel said, interrupting my thoughts.

"That's cool. I mean; nice to meet ya, Hannah."

I put up a hand as if to wave, then, felt a little awkward until she mirrored my action and waved back. Without waiting for an invite, I stepped onto the porch to join the others.

Hannah picked up a pitcher from a long table in front of a set of windows that lined the front of the house along the length of the porch. "Would you like some lemonade?"

"Yep. That would be nice. I just gave mine away to my brother in the south field a few minutes ago, and completely forgot to get myself some more. I'm awful thirsty," I rattled on nervously.

Talking to people that I didn't know had never been a talent of mine, but after the conversation I just had with Mitchell, I figured it was time for me to learn.

"Oh no!"

Rachel startled me with her sudden outburst.

"I knew I would forget to take a drink to Papa and Elijah. *Mam's* going to give me extra chores if I don't get out there."

Rachel scampered a bit to gather the glasses full of refreshment for the two in the field.

"I'll help ya," I offered, secretly hoping this might be my chance to speak to the boy I admired so.

"Well, let's go if we're going to do it," Hannah said.

Until that moment, I hadn't counted on it being a group outing, feeling a little unsure of myself. I didn't want an audience when I met up with Elijah in the field, but it was too late to rethink my offer of service.

I followed nervously behind the three girls, trying not to spill the pitcher that held the remaining lemonade in it. When Elijah came into view, a lump welled up in my throat, making it difficult to breathe. Once again, I found myself trudging over clumps of dirt—only this time I had to manage a half-full pitcher of lemonade instead of a mere glass. My eyes locked onto Elijah's, and even from that distance, I could see the deep blue of his eyes as they sparkled in the sun.

Without warning, my foot caught in a clump of earth, sending me face down in the dirt. My ankle had twisted in the dirt, causing me to let out a high-pitched yelp just prior to landing. Lemonade seemed to spray in every direction, especially in my hair. Elijah immediately ran to my aid, but I was so embarrassed, I found it difficult to look him in the eye. I suddenly tasted blood mixed with the dirt in my mouth.

Rachel gasped. "You're bleeding, Miss Jane!"

"Take her on up to the house, Elijah." Mr. Zook spoke with authority.

Elijah offered his arm in assistance, which was a bit awkward in the beginning. However, the shooting pain in my ankle was bigger than my pride at the moment, which forced me to accept his arm with gratitude. He seemed to be a knowledgeable and calm guide, but I supposed he'd seen worse injuries on the farm than my ankle.

"Steady now," he cautioned. "You don't have to hurry. I imagine you'll be off that ankle for a *gut* while."

His voice was as gentle as I'd imagined it to be, and his strength in holding me was exciting. I was in no hurry, I felt safe and secure with his strong arms around me. We arrived at the porch of his farmhouse, and he sat me down gently in the same worn porch swing that Rachel had sat in just minutes before. Then he reached up and smoothed back my sticky hair from my face and smiled a heartfelt smile.

"Looks like ya got yourself a mouthful of my God-given earth, and it's smudged your pretty face a little, too," he said.

My face flushed at his boldness.

Does he really think I'm pretty, or is he just being nice? I don't think I care. I just like the attention.

Ha…equal rights are for ugly girls.

Though I knew it wasn't right to get caught up in his good looks, I couldn't help myself. I had to admit, though, his kindness was enough to make this moment worth the world to me, and I was prepared to milk it for all its worth.

"You wait here, Jane, and I'll get a wet cloth to mop up some of the blood."

I stared into his smiling blue eyes until he turned and walked away. All my life I had despised my name, until Elijah spoke it just then. Up until recently, my mother had spoken my name in harshness, but it sounded almost poetic coming from his lips.

When he returned, he sat down beside me on the swing, and began to dab gently at my bleeding lip. I studied his bright blue eyes, hoping for a sign that his kind actions weren't out of some sort of Amish tradition. My father had told us about the people's kindness being "their way", but I wanted to believe this was more than traditional Amish kindness. Neither of us said a word, but I felt as though there was plenty being said as we fixed our eyes on one another. I wanted to kiss him. I'd always been an impulsive person, but my bloody lip kept the desire in check. My awkwardness had left me, and a sense of belonging settled in me as we sat quietly starring at each other for what seemed like a slow-moving moment in time.

Rachel and Lucy broke the silence when they scampered up onto the porch steps. Rachel even sat between us on the swing. I leered at her, knowing she did it on purpose. Elijah stood up abruptly and took my hand in his. His hands were rough and worn, as though they had seen many days of hard labor.

"Is there anything else you need, Jane?"

His manner was so gentle that I wanted to beg him to stay, but I held my tongue.

"Papa will be missing me in the fields, I should get back," he said, his hands still clenching mine.

He flashed me a smile as he let my hand down gently in my lap. He advanced to the steps of the porch and turned to leave.

I understood he had work to do, but I didn't like it. When he turned back, I sensed his hesitation.

"I'll be fine," I said, shooing him with my hand. "I just bruised my pride a little."

He stood there smiling at me as though he understood, then, stepped off the porch, heading back toward the field. He turned his head a final time before leaving the yard to wave, and I waved back, feeling confident that this was the beginning of a friendship that might prove to be greater than the ones I had with Bradley and Penelope.

"I'll stop by to see you tomorrow, if it's okay with you?" he asked.

I wanted to jump up with excitement, but my ankle kept me in check. So I nodded my answer with a smile, and watched him disappear beyond the pine trees that surrounded the porch. I was suddenly thankful for the reminder of the pain in my ankle, which forced me to act like a lady instead of being impulsive the way I had been most of my life. If I was to win his heart I may have to begin to mimic the girls whose company I was presently keeping.

"Elijah likes you," Rachel teased.

Hannah made kissing noises against her hand. "Is there anything else you need, Jane?"

"Don't mock me," I insisted.

"I can't help it. It was just so cute the way he took your hand in his. I agree with Rachel. I believe my cousin likes you."

I looked at Hannah, wondering if she was still teasing me, or if she truly believed Elijah liked me. Excitement welled up in me, and I was almost glad I'd fallen.

ଅଓ

That night, I could scarcely sleep. I tossed and fidgeted so often that I woke Nadine.

"What's the matter with ya? Go back to sleep and be quiet."

"Don't yell at me, Nadine."

"If I was yellin', you'd know it," she threatened.

"Ya are so yellin', so cut it out."

"Nope. And you can't make me."

"I'm sorry, Nadine. Don't be mad at me. I didn't mean to wake ya. I just can't stop thinkin' 'bout Elijah."

She raised a thin eyebrow and sat up in her bed to face me.

"What about Elijah?" She was practically gritting her teeth when she spoke.

"Oh man. I've never been so embarrassed in my whole life as I was today. I fell in Elijah's field and he had to help me back to his porch. But oh my gosh, Elijah was so sweet to me. Ya wouldn't believe how nice he is—and so cute too, but anyone can see that."

Nadine sighed and rolled her eyes, stuffing her pillow over her head.

"I'm just so happy that ya got to spend time with him, but I don't want to hear another word, so please shut up and go back to sleep," came a muffled and angry scolding from Nadine.

"Well ya don't sound very happy for me. What're ya gettin' so mad about?"

Nadine yanked the pillow off her face and pursed her lips. "Not another word, Jane—I mean it."

"What's yer problem, Nadine? Yer actin' like yer jealous."

"I am not jealous. I just want ya to stop talkin' and go back to sleep."

"Yer the one that needs to stop talking. If ya don't be quiet, yer gonna wake up everybody in the house," I warned her.

"I said not another word or you'll be sorry—I mean it, Jane—this is yer last warning."

"You need to take a chill-pill," I said, throwing a stuffed animal at her. I laid down on my bed, determined to dream of Elijah—she certainly couldn't stop me from doing that.

∞∞

The following morning, my ankle was very stiff and hurt more than the day before. It reminded me of a time when I was five, and had sprained my ankle because my mother had let me fall from the monkey bars at my elementary school. She had been so cruel that day by teasing me and refusing to help me down.

As I hobbled down the stairs, I reminded myself that I'd forgiven my mother quite some time ago, so I determined that I would put it out of my mind. I smiled as I reflected on the day she came home from the clinic, but a sudden commotion toward the side of the house interrupted my thoughts.

When I opened the door, I was surprised to see Elijah with a horse.

"Hello, Miss Jane."

He tipped his hat and bowed slightly, making me feel somewhat bashful.

"I felt so awful about what happened yesterday, that I took it upon myself to bring my horse, Eli, to be your personal escort to school for the next few days."

His tone was very polite, but also very formal. I was stunned by his offer even though I was happy at the thought of being able to have some time to get to know him better.

"Wait a minute while I grab my sweater," I said from over my shoulder.

The excuse of needing a sweater would give me enough time to rid myself of the giddiness I felt. After all, I couldn't afford any more embarrassment. When I re-entered the house through the side door, Nadine was pacing the wooden floors of the front room. She stormed over to me and suddenly grabbed my arm and squeezed tightly.

"What's Elijah doin' here?"

"What're ya mad at me, for? He only brought his horse over to give me a ride to school. Leave me alone. I ain't gonna fight with ya anymore." I pulled my arm away from her.

"I'm goin' with you. Papa will say it'll look improper for you to go alone."

"Oh now it's "*Papa*", is it? What're ya gonna do? Tell Mom and Dad on me if I refuse?" I challenged her.

"What if I do?"

I shrugged, and looked down at the floor, feeling defeated.

"I knew you'd see it my way," she said. "So I guess ya won't be arguing with me anymore about goin' with ya."

Her statement was final, and I knew she was probably right. It angered me, though; because I knew her reasons for going were partly out of jealousy. We walked out the side door together, and met Elijah on the dirt drive.

"Nadine will be hangin' with us," I announced.

"Are ya all right, Jane? Ya seem a little upset." Elijah tried making eye contact with me, but I didn't want him to see the fury in my eyes.

"I'm cool," I muttered softly.

It was a lie, but I couldn't burden a new friend with the petty problems between Nadine and me—especially since he was the subject of our dispute. Elijah seemed to pick up on my annoyance with the situation, but smiled softly at me.

"Why don't the two of you ride, and I'll walk alongside. There certainly isn't enough room on this horse for the three of us," he said.

There wouldn't be three of us if my sister wasn't so bossy and controlling.

We laughed lightly, alleviating some of the tension between my sister and me. He assisted the two of us onto Eli, which was slightly awkward at first, being our first time on a horse. Nadine took full advantage of his assistance, using the opportunity to flirt with *my* Elijah. Even though he hadn't made known his intentions toward me, I still felt that we were meant for one another, just from the way he looked at me. Along the way, Nadine monopolized nearly the entire conversation, causing anger to rise in me like it hadn't in years. I pushed aside the angry thoughts, hoping Elijah wouldn't pick up on it.

When we finally reached the schoolhouse, I was so eager to be rid of my sister that I decided I should remain outside for a minute to put a halt to my fuming. Elijah must have finally noticed my agitation, for he stalled in giving assistance to us in dismounting the horse.

Nadine, in her impatience, tried showing off by trying to dismount the horse on her own, and fell to the ground in her unsuccessful attempt. Unable to hold in my anger any longer, I let out the most un-lady-like guffaw, but quickly apologized. Nadine ignored my apology and pushed aside the hand that Elijah offered. She dusted herself off, then, stormed into the school. This left me to deal with my guilt and embarrassment in facing Elijah's silence alone. If ever I was to get off on the wrong foot with someone, the embarrassment of strife between Nadine and me didn't present well. How could I ever convince him that I could be the one for him after what he just witnessed?

"I'd like to say a prayer for the two of you," he said after a minute or so.

I was shocked by his offer. I thought he would walk away from me after I'd been so unsympathetic toward my sister. Still, he looked at me with kindness showing in his eyes.

"My father told me that there's differences in our beliefs—not just the way we live." I stumbled over my words.

"My papa was brought up in the Old Order, and I was, too, until five years ago. My father's relatives in Pennsylvania brought about the change under the leadership of their Bishop. Now we embrace even more liberal ways in our *Ordnung*."

I knew if we didn't end our conversation soon, I would be tardy, but I didn't want to go in and leave things the way they were.

"May I say a prayer for you anyway?" he asked humbly.

I nodded my approval and he urged me to go into the schoolhouse. I stalled for a minute to watch from the top step as he rode away in a cloud of dust on Eli.

THREE
A TIME TO MATURE

After school, Elijah was there to pick me up, just as he had promised. I didn't want Nadine tagging along this time and wondered how I could rid myself of her. I'd spent a fair portion of my afternoon thinking up excuses, but had neglected to see the obvious until she nudged me at the top of the stairs at the schoolhouse.

"Hey, watch it. Ya almost knocked me down the steps."

"Don't be so dramatic, Jane. I only wanted to tell ya that I'm not ridin' on that horse again."

"Does that mean you're gonna rat on me if I do?"

"No, Jane. I ain't gonna rat on ya. As long as ya stop actin' like you're so happy to get rid of me."

"I'm not happy to get rid of you."

Peace out.

"Just don't get caught by *The Man*, or you'll be grounded for life."

"Nadine, thanks for being so cool about this. I'm really sorry for the mean things that I said to ya last night. And I didn't mean to wake ya up."

"I forgive ya. I'm sorry too. Hey, I'll see ya back home."

"Bye, Nadine."

I was happy that Nadine and I had settled our differences, but much happier that she'd opted out of the ride home on Elijah's horse. Elijah showed up just then and called me over to him with a wave of his hand, causing most of the girls in the schoolyard to gasp. I looked back at them and the looks of envy on their faces.

Keep your eyes in your heads girls because that fox is mine.

Seeing their envious faces gave me an additional boost in confidence. I gave Hannah a quick "thumbs-up" and limped slightly in my walk over to Elijah, then, allowed him to boost me up on the horse. He walked quietly beside me for several minutes, until I thought I could no longer stand the silence.

"It doesn't seem right that I should ride and you should walk. I don't mind if ya wanna ride with me," I said.

"Ya don't sound too sure about your offer."

I'm perfectly sure I want you closer to me, daring me in ways I ought not to be thinking about.

"Well, I wasn't sure how ya might take it. I'd like it if you'd ride with me—maybe so we could go a little faster on him."

"*Jah*, but it might not look *gut* to your papa if he should see us on the horse together."

"Does that mean ya don't wanna ride with me?"

"No, Jane. I'd like to ride with ya—show ya how fast he can go. I'm just not sure that it would be proper."

Right now I don't care what my father would think.

"My father is at work in town, he won't see us. Let's just be keepin' it real. I won't tell him if you won't."

"Are ya asking me to keep it a secret?" Elijah flashed me a crooked grin.

Oh how that smile turns me on.

"Maybe. B'sides, it ain't like we're doin' anything wrong, so he'll be cool with it even if he does find out."

I lied.

If the truth be told, my father—papa—would likely have forbidden me to see Elijah again if he were to catch me riding the horse with him. I knew it was wrong to keep silent about my father's rules, but my desire to have Elijah near me was clouding my judgment of what the exact truth was. It was my opinion that I was plenty old enough to ride a horse with a boy. After all, it was my father who had changed his mind regarding the age Nadine and I could begin dating. If he challenged me my argument would be that Elijah and I were just friends...even though I intended to try for more.

Long before we moved into the Amish community, he sat us down and told us he would like us to mirror the rules of proper behavior after our new neighbors. At the time, neither of us cared if we had to wait an extra year to date because neither of us had any real prospects.

"There ain't nothin' but Amish boys out in the wilderness where yer takin' us, so why should we care?" Nadine had said at the time.

If only I had known about Elijah before I agreed to such a rule. Now the only question was; how could I weasel my way out of this one?

Elijah flashed me a quick smile of acceptance to my offer, then mounted the horse, and settled in behind me. I pushed my thoughts of getting caught aside when his arms went around me as he grabbed the reigns. I was grateful that he was behind me; unable to see my face flush when his arms went around me. Eli bucked slightly, showing his protest at having two riders on his back. I squealed a little out of fear and grabbed Elijah's arms to brace myself. Strong arms tightened around me, keeping me on the horse, as I fell back against Elijah's chest. When the horse settled down and began a slow trot, I relaxed just enough to start a conversation in an attempt to break the awkward silence.

"Is this your horse, or does it belong to your papa?"

"Being the oldest son, I get my own horse, but I would guess that Samuel will get one, too. Papa's *gut* and generous," he said. "I own a pig and a cow too. Papa gave them to me when I was younger, to test my abilities with the farm stock."

There was another long silence in which my thoughts wandered to my riding companion. I had allowed myself to remain up against his broad, muscular frame and it seemed somewhat confusing that he didn't protest.

"Does this make us friends?"

His question interrupted my thoughts and my face felt hot as I wondered if he was referring to the fact that I hadn't stopped leaning on him. I sat up straight out of embarrassment.

"What do ya mean?" I asked nervously.

"I wondered if we'll be friends now that we'll be spending a *gut* amount of time together. After all, I'll be escorting you to school until your ankle is healed."

"I suppose it does," I said quietly.

"In that case, I'm happy to be your friend. My other friends might even accuse me of *rumspringa,*" he said, then, laughed out loud.

"Uh—wait a minute. What does that mean?"

"Don't worry. It isn't anything bad. It means to run around together—with a girl—to be friends with her. I thought we could be friends—secretly, perhaps. To avoid having the fellas tease me," he said.

It sounded as though he was saying the same things that Mitchell was saying about he and Rebekah. I didn't understand most of Elijah's explanation, but was relieved that he hadn't mentioned my improper actions. I liked being close to Elijah, and wondered if the horse might buck again just so I would get another opportunity to lean up against him.

"I'd like it if we could be friends, and I'll even be happy to keep it our little secret," I said.

Truth was; I couldn't keep a secret. But I no longer had anyone to tell. Putting it in a letter and sending it to the girls at school wasn't the same as seeing their reaction if I told them in person. Besides, they would probably tease me because they just wouldn't understand being attracted to an Amish boy. Though he wasn't what I expected, there was no way I could convince city girls that Elijah fit into the category of "fox".

I looked back at him over my shoulder. Who cares if I had no one to tell? My heart raced at the thought of being his girl.

I was painfully aware that friendship was all I could have for the time being, because friendship was all he was offering. I didn't dare tell him that I'd thought ahead about what it would be like to be married to him some day—that would be a foolish thing to blurt out. In spite of my feelings, he had expressed only friendship, so I made up my mind to be content with the relationship he offered. I looked back at him again in time to catch the full smile that played gently across his lips.

When we reached the property line, I slid down from the horse with assistance from my riding companion. Elijah then bid me good-bye with a tip of his hat and a promise to return promptly in the morning. So formal and proper, I wasn't sure what to do but nod back in fear that my hippie talk would scare him off. Being the gentleman he was, he just smiled at me.

Filled with excitement, I practically skipped into the house, forgetting that my ankle was still swollen and in need of rest. My mother and Naomi were bursting with excitement as I entered the front room.

"We have a surprise for you," Naomi said.

I glanced at my mother, unsure of whether I was in for a lecture or the surprise she looked eager to share.

"I'm in kind of a hurry, Mamma, I forgot to get the eggs outta the hen house this mornin'."

"I got them after you left for school, and you can have a few days off until your ankle heals. Now come sit down—this is important, Jane."

I plopped down on the coffee table, realizing by the look on Naomi's face, she didn't think it proper to sit the way I was, or address my mother the way I had. A twinge of worry passed through me, but only because I didn't want her telling Elijah; so I stood up and spoke to my mother in a more polite tone.

To my surprise, she presented me with a long dress that resembled the one Hannah had worn the day before. I was so thrilled that I twirled with a limp around the room, holding the dress up against the front of me. I couldn't wait to wear it tomorrow to school. Then I thought of Elijah, and wondered if he would approve.

Of course he would. This would give me just the opportunity I needed to show him how adaptable I was to his way of life.

Nadine entered through the front door at that time, and protested the dressmaking. Lucy and Rachel admired their new dresses, and Molly modeled hers for us. We all laughed, save Nadine, when Molly's chubby little frame curtsied.

"I don't wanna dress this way, mother," Nadine said loudly.

Any time Nadine was angry, she referred to our parents as "mother" or "father" with disrespect in her tone.

"Anna, you really shouldn't let her speak to you in that tone," Naomi said.

You tell her Naomi. Nadine needs her mouth washed out with soap.

"Nadine, you'll get used to this sort of dress. Besides, all the girls at school will be dressed the same, so you won't risk being teased." My mother's tone was gentle despite Nadine's disrespectful undertones.

"*Mam*, please don't make me wear that stuff."

It always amazed me how quickly Nadine could change her tone when she wanted to win an argument. Sometimes she could be so conniving and disrespectful. I don't know why my mother put up with it.

"I won't force you, Nadine," my mother said. "But I hope that you'll reconsider."

I couldn't take it anymore. The fake fight they were having for the sake of Naomi was making me sick.

"Yer so spoiled and ungrateful, Nadine."

"Stop yellin' at me, Jane. Just because you happen to like yer dress, doesn't mean that I have to like mine. I just don't like wearin' dresses. I'm not Amish and I'm not gonna dress like I am."

"Ya don't like wearin' dresses 'cause yer really a boy, Nadine."

"Take that back, Jane, or you'll be sorry."

"Stop trippin', Nadine. Maybe ya *need* to wear a dress. Since ya cut yer hair so short ya look even more like Mitchell. The two of ya could be twins."

"Take it back Jane, or I'm gonna cut yer hair in yer sleep. Then we'll see who looks like a boy."

"I don't have to take anything back, Nadine. I ain't afraid of you. Ya need to be thankful instead of bein' so hateful. I like my new threads 'cause it beats wearin' Cousin Shelly's old hand-me-downs any day."

By this time we were shouting and I immediately regretted acting like that in front of Elijah's mother, fearing she might tell him everything.

My mother stood between us. "Now, girls. Stop your bickering. I'm sure we can work this out somehow," she said calmly.

Though I could see how annoyed my mother was, having her treat us with patience was something I was still getting used to. Back when she would drink, she'd usually hit us before we even got a chance to argue. But at this point, I wasn't sure if the only reason she was holding back was because we had company. Either way, I was done listening to Nadine's spoiled tantrum, when it was obvious to everyone how much my mother was trying to make amends.

Nadine ignored my mother's plea for peace and stamped her feet as she ran off bawling. Naomi gave my mother a stern look, causing her to apologize for our un-lady-like tones.

ଏଠଔଷ

In the morning, I heard Elijah arrive at the side door with Eli as I finished fastening the pale green calico dress that my mamma had so lovingly made for me. I had to admit that I appreciated my mother's efforts at trying to make up for what she'd put us all through—it was really nice having a mother again.

The clip-clop of the horse's hooves sounded louder than yesterday, but I didn't think much of it. The house was quiet since my mother and younger siblings were still asleep, and my father had left for work nearly an hour before. When I opened the door, I discovered what all the commotion was from; there was another boy and another horse waiting with Elijah and Eli.

"Jane, you look wonderful *gut* in that dress," Elijah said.

His face turned a slight shade of red as his eyes looked toward the ground.

"*Ach*, I really didn't mean to encourage vanity or anything," he said in his defense. "It's just that you could almost pass for an Amish girl, *jah!*"

He stared at me for just a minute, then, seemingly caught himself.

"This is Benjamin Lapp. He's Hannah's older brother."

Benjamin moved forward and tipped his hat at his introduction.

"I would like to take Nadine to school if she'll allow me to escort her. Is she still here?" Benjamin asked slowly.

I let out a whoop, then, checked myself by placing a hand over my mouth. I was so excited at the possibility that

I could be rid of Nadine, that I was certainly ready to hand her over to this other boy.

"If you'll excuse me for a minute, I'll go see if she'll accept an escort today," I said, using my best manners.

After excusing myself, I limped back into the house to look for Nadine. I found her checking her hair in the mirror above the piano in the front room. I stood waiting for a moment, then, approached her cautiously.

"There's a boy outside with his horse. He'd like to escort ya to school—his words, not mine," I said, trying to keep from laughing.

"Elijah's here for me?"

"You can wipe the smile off your face, 'cause it ain't Elijah—he's here too, but he ain't here for you," I said harshly.

"Who is it, then?"

"He's Hannah Lapp's older brother, Benjamin," I said.

"Is he cute?"

"Is that all ya care about, Nadine?"

"Well, is he?" she insisted.

"I suppose he's sorta cute, but Dad wouldn't approve of ya bein' so shallow. B'sides," I said. "He's not nearly as handsome as Elijah."

After making that statement, I realized how foolish it was to encourage Nadine to see Elijah in the same manner I did, so I quickly tried to retract my statement.

"You might think Benjamin's a total fox. Ya know we usually have different taste in everything—why should our taste in how cute a boy is be any different?" I asked, trying to recover from my previously foolish remark.

Nadine eagerly took the bait and followed me to get a look at her would-be caller. I opened the door and she stuck her head out so I could introduce her to Benjamin.

"Uh—excuse me just a minute, I'll be right back," she said, then, ran abruptly into the house.

I wondered what she was up to, but kept silent as I allowed Elijah to boost me up onto Eli. It was a more difficult task than it had been the previous day, due to having to ride sidesaddle because of my long dress. Elijah then mounted the horse behind me, and we waited to see if Nadine would return. When she did, she had on the dress that *Mam* had sewn for her, instead of her favorite pair of worn trousers. My mouth hung open in amazement at the sight of Nadine in the pale blue dress with the starched, white collar.

It's too bad Mamma ain't awake to see this 'cause she would really get a kick out seein' Nadine flaunting the dress she swore she'd never wear. I can't wait 'till she gets a good look at her after school.

My mother had never been a morning person, but lately the increasing girth of her pregnancy kept her in bed most mornings until well after eight o'clock.

"I hope I didn't take too much time in getting ready," she said, giggling in Benjamin's direction. "I'd enjoy havin' ya escort me, thank you."

Her sudden politeness was enough to make me ill, but I held my tongue, not wanting to cause her any more embarrassment—she was already doing a fine job of it herself. Benjamin helped her onto his horse as she pretended to be helpless. He didn't get on the large beast with her, but merely clicked a command to the horse and walked along beside her.

Since Elijah and I were riding together, we went ahead of Benjamin and Nadine; which suited me just fine. I was certain I wouldn't be able to hold my tongue any longer if I had to continue to listen to her schoolgirl giggling.

છ૭જી

A dense fog filtered through the tall grass and intermittently scattered itself among the trail. The air was crisp, though not cold enough to give me a chill. Once again, I allowed myself to lean into Elijah's chest as we rode along, though not as much as the previous day. I tried convincing myself I was just trying to keep warm—or maybe I was already creating an alibi in case Elijah questioned me.

Elijah startled me by touching the back of my hair. His hand caused me to shiver as he ran his hand underneath my hair and touched my neck softly. He lifted the back of my hair with his free hand and pushed it to the top of my head.

"Your hair would be beautiful up on your head. Maybe with little curls falling alongside your face," he said.

His touch and his words made me feel suddenly very impulsive. I wanted him to kiss me, but I tried to keep my feelings in check. I preferred my hair down, and allowing it to fly in the breeze as the horse galloped along made me feel very free. I was, however, willing to wear it in a fashion that would please Elijah.

"Maybe I'll pin it up tomorrow—just to see how it looks," I said enthusiastically.

"*Ach*, ya don't have to do that for me. If ya did, though, it would almost make ya seem like you were my girl—more like my *maidel*."

"There ya go again, usin' foreign words I don't understand," I said, poking his ribs with my elbow.

"It means a girl that's not married."

I didn't know what to say. I felt both confusion and excitement, but I didn't dare question his meaning. I didn't want him thinking I was incapable of comprehending his seemingly simple statement. He said I was his girl, and I would accept it at face value—even though it did sound cooler in a foreign language. I merely sighed and leaned a little further into his broad frame. Elijah cradled me gently in his arms as he slowed the horse a little. Then we veered off the trail and Elijah hopped off the horse to pick some wild flowers. When he handed them to me, I blushed slightly, then, fumbled a comment about getting to school before the bell rang. It seemed unreal to me that I could feel this deeply for a boy that I'd spent only a few days with, but I knew I already loved him.

As we trotted along, the schoolhouse came into view all too soon and I felt disappointment as he took my hand to ease me off of his horse. Benjamin and Nadine had beaten us there and were standing in the shade of the big oak tree in the schoolyard. They seemed to be keeping a joyful sort of conversation between them and this pleased me. Elijah led Eli around to face the opposite direction, as he promised me his return after school. His clutch on my hand lingered as our eyes locked, but I knew our time together had ended.

With the clanging of the bell that hung on the outside of the schoolhouse, he hopped back on Eli and rode away at a fast gallop. Hannah met me at the bench that we shared in the large schoolroom. Her kindness made me wonder why I'd been so reluctant in making friends when my family first moved to the rural community. I disliked the idea of leaving the friends I'd had all my life, and initially I resented my parent's decision to move me so far away from civilization as I knew it. But looking at Hannah made me realize that the purity of this lifestyle was something I'd been craving all my life. Mitchell had been right in saying that I needed to put my energy toward the friends I now had instead of mourning over the ones I'd lost in the move. Things were moving fast and for the better, and I was beginning to feel grateful for the change in circumstances.

Hannah nudged me out of my thoughts.

"How are ya getting along with my cousin, Elijah?" she asked.

I felt warmth rising in my cheeks as I thought about Elijah, but I tried desperately not to let it show.

"He's every bit a gentleman—and he has a beautiful horse."

I didn't dare say any more for fear that I would give away my true feelings.

"My brother, Benjamin, says that you are all Elijah talks about these last few days. I think he wants to court ya."

My hands shook and my heart beat faster as she stared at me, waiting for a response. I wasn't prepared to share my true feelings about Elijah with anyone yet.

"I'm afraid I can't have a real caller 'til I'm seventeen, and I'm only fifteen now," I complained.

"When will ya be sixteen?"

"Not 'till next month—October fourth."

Hannah gasped as though I'd said something wrong, and I looked at her, waiting for her to explain.

"Elijah's birthday is October fourth," she said with wide eyes.

"Wow, that's cool. That means he turned one year old when I was born! That is so cool that we have the same birthday!"

Won't he be surprised when I tell him after school?

&❦&

The school day slowly came to an end, and I could hardly wait for my ride home with Elijah. When I walked out of the school, though, he wasn't waiting for me outside like he had the day prior. Worry rose up in me that he'd changed his mind about his feelings. I sat down on the steep wooden steps that led into the school, determined that he would eventually show up. With a sigh, Hannah sat down beside me.

"Ya want me to wait with ya?" she asked.

Nadine walked out of the school just then, and it seemed that she was looking for Benjamin also.

"Nadine can wait with me, but thanks for the offer, Hannah. I'll try to come over later and work some on shuckin' corn if ya'd like me to."

"Sure could use the help. *Denki*. I'll see ya later if ya have the time, Jane."

She walked slowly toward the lane that led to her farmhouse. I wasn't sure I wanted to shuck corn, but I was certain I wanted a friend, and I hoped I'd get the time to go over to her house and help her.

Nadine flashed me an impatient look, as though she wanted me to get rid of Hannah—and fast.

"What gives?" I asked.

"What do ya mean—what gives?"

"Ya know exactly what. What do ya want?"

"Look, Jane, I know we haven't been gettin' along too good lately, but I really need to talk to ya."

She was almost in tears.

"What's wrong?"

"Benjamin asked if he could call on me," Nadine blurted out. "What should I do, and how should I answer him?"

Nadine seemed to be in a sort of panic.

"Gee whiz, those Amish boys don't waste any time, do they?"

"This one didn't. What am I supposed to do, Jane?"

"Do ya think you're interested? I mean, if ya court him, ya probably have to marry him when you're done."

My words sounded final—even to myself, and Nadine looked a little pale after I said it.

"I'm confused. I mean, no offense, Jane, but yesterday I thought I wanted to steal Elijah from you, and then this morning when I saw Benjamin—oh, he's so cute, and very nice. I even wore this dumb dress to impress him, but I don't wanna marry anybody. Not right now, I'm only sixteen," she said, sounding a little desperate.

"Dad says proper courtin' can take a year or more. That'll give ya plenty of time to get used to the idea."

"That's not funny, Jane. Don't tease me."

"Don't freak out at me for tellin' the truth. Just be cool and think about this logically as Dad would tell ya to do."

"This is a tough one to answer. He's seventeen already, and he'll be expectin' me to marry him if I let him call on me."

"So what did ya tell him?"

I was almost too curious to wait for an answer.

"I told him I couldn't officially court for another ten days when I turn seventeen, hoping that would buy me a little more time to get to know him before I make up my mind. Do ya think we're too young and immature to get married so young like these Amish boys are used to?"

"No way, Nadine. After everything we've had to deal with so far in life, we're probably way more mature than any Amish girl twice our age."

"I guess you're right, Jane. But I worry that Benjamin won't wait long, though. Rebekah told me that Deborah Yoder is sweet on him. I'm guessing that means she likes him too."

Who knew Amish girls could be so competitive?

"I'm not sure I'd worry about her—she likes most every Amish boy around here. Do ya think he likes her?"

"I don't think he'd ask me to the youth singin' next Sunday if he liked Deborah—do you?"

She sounded almost worried.

I heard the clip clop of the horses and looked up to see Benjamin and Elijah riding side by side toward the schoolhouse.

"Here's your chance to ask him," I said as I got up to meet Elijah.

"I don't know if I can do this, Jane."

"Well ya better hurry up and think of somethin' to say to him," I warned her.

They both rode up to the steps and helped us on their horses. Benjamin didn't get on with Nadine this time either, and she flashed me a look of desperation. I knew she wanted my help, but I rode off with Elijah holding me tight. I didn't dare look back because I was too involved in my own dilemma.

"Sorry we were late." Elijah said. "We were in town helping your *papa* and Mitchell get some supplies at the feed store."

"That's cool; it gave me and Nadine a chance to talk over a few things."

"Did ya settle your differences?"

"Yeah, but Nadine just told me what Benjamin's intentions are for her. Did ya know anything about this?"

"*Jah*, I already knew," he admitted.

"Don't ya think it's sorta sudden?"

I wasn't prepared for Elijah's answer, but he stated the embarrassing truth regardless of my readiness to hear it.

"While you and Nadine were busy watching me and my papa in our field for the last few weeks," he said slowly, trying to suppress a grin. "Benjamin was watching Nadine from his field that runs alongside ours."

My face was so flushed by the time he finished—I couldn't even look at him. I buried my head against his chest and closed my eyes; unable to deny what he had said—I could only offer an apology.

"I am so embarrassed, and so sorry that we spied on ya like that." I hung my head, not wanting to face him in my humiliation.

"I'm not sorry. I'm flattered."

He gave me a quick squeeze that felt more like a hug, but I wasn't about to question it.

"So ya think she should tell him yes?"

"Jane, you have a one-track mind don't ya?"

I turned back and looked him in the eye, trying to establish whether he was getting impatient with me. When he smiled, I offered a pleading look, but he didn't take the hint.

"Well? Tell me what ya think. Please."

"She should say what she feels. But you should warn her not to take too long in answering if she's also interested in him."

"Why?"

"I happen to know that Deborah Yoder has been sweet on him for two years. Until Nadine showed up, he thought he was going to have to settle for her. If she turns him down, he'll likely marry Deborah."

"That seems a little harsh, don't ya think?"

"It probably is, but that's how he feels. I don't think she wants him to marry Deborah if she takes too long in deciding. She may change her mind later, but then it would be too late. He wants to be married soon, and he wants it to be Nadine," he said.

"She was afraid of that. I hope she doesn't choose outta fear of losin' him. She doesn't hardly know him."

We both let out a heavy sigh at the same time.

"Ya won't tease him will ya? For courtin', I mean."

"Benjamin Lapp isn't just my cousin, he's my best friend. We wouldn't tease each other about that. We'll leave that to the less mature boys who attend the Singings."

Elijah gave me another gentle squeeze, and I remained silent the rest of the trip, as I wondered how long it would be before I'd be able to attend a Singing with him.

FOUR
A TIME OF TESTING

Elijah didn't take me home. Instead, he steered the horse toward his own barn. Mitchell was waiting on a milking stool just inside the barn when we rode up.

He stood up to greet us

"Elijah, I hope your intentions toward my sister are strictly proper," he said.

"Mitchell, don't get after him like you're my father."

"You stay outta this, Jane. I'm talkin' to Elijah, not you."

"Don't worry so much, Mitchell, I'm not out to hurt her. I care for her and my intentions are *gut*."

They were discussing me as though I wasn't there, and it angered me slightly, until what Elijah said registered in my brain. I smiled wide, unable to prevent the grin from spreading across my face—my cheeks aching from grinning so wide.

"If ya expect me to believe that your intentions are proper toward Jane, then I shouldn't catch you riding that horse with her again," Mitchell said sternly.

Elijah nodded his agreement. I was so mad at Mitchell I wanted to spit, but I held my tongue. No, I would wait until after Elijah left to discuss my displeasure over my brother's treatment of me.

After giving his horse a good long drink, Elijah put Eli in his stall, and turned his attention to Mitchell. He was trying to explain the right way to take care of a barn to prepare Mitchell to handle the few heads of cattle he and my father had purchased earlier in the week. When it came time to explain the milking of the cow, my brother got a little squeamish. Up until they purchased the milk cow, we'd been getting our milk in town from Fork's General Store. I was interested in seeing the show, so I sat still in the haystack, observing Mitchell's clumsiness.

"*Ach*, if you're ever to marry my sister, ya better let me teach ya how to be a real farmer," Elijah said, jokingly.

"Stop laughin' at me. I seriously need to learn this stuff," Mitchell said.

"There's a lot more to farming than running that fancy tractor of yours back and forth along the soil," Benjamin teased as he entered the barn.

Upon hearing his cheerful voice, I wondered how the ride home had been between Nadine and him. I was concerned that Nadine may need to have a talk, but I wasn't willing to leave just yet and miss out on Mitchell's lessons. In an effort to divert my attention from the laughter, I pushed playfully at one of the barn cats, pretending not to notice the two of them poking fun at my brother.

"May I give it a try?" I asked politely, after tiring of hearing my brother complaining.

Elijah motioned for me to take Mitchell's place at the milking stool, and he crouched behind me to guide my hands to the cow's udder.

"I'm leaving," Mitchell said. "You two lovebirds are enough to make a fella sick."

I sighed heavily as my brother stormed off, my face flush from his forward statements. Benjamin was already on my brother's heels, calling after him and begging him not to give up so easily.

"Is that what we are? Lovebirds?" Elijah asked around a grin wide enough to expose the dimples in both his cheeks.

I thought about how he expected me to answer such a question, then, decided to give my honest opinion.

"We are as long as no one finds out just yet," I said.

His grin widened as he nodded his head and rested his chin on my shoulder, allowing his cheek to touch mine as we milked the cow together.

ଔଔ

Later, I caught up to Nadine, who had decided that my side of our bedroom needed to be as clean as her side. Whenever Nadine was upset about something, she would clean, and I would end up having to suffer for it by cleaning my side of the room to match hers. Normally, I would pace, nearly wearing a hole in the floor, if I had a crisis, but I was too happy to pace or to argue with her about cleaning the room.

"What're you so happy about?"

"Me? Uh, uh," I stammered.

"Somethin's goin' on with you and Elijah, ain't it?"

"I can't say anything, Nadine, or Dad will find out."

"Who's gonna rat on ya, Jane?"

"Mitchell threatened to. He saw us ridin' on the horse together."

"Mitchell ain't a nark; he won't rat on ya. He's just trying to scare ya."

"Ya think so?" I asked.

"Don't worry so much about it. He ain't gonna tell. Just don't let him see ya on the horse with Elijah anymore, or he might be tempted."

"When did he turn into such a goody-two-shoes?"

"I think somethin' changed in him when mom came home from the drunk-tank."

"Don't say that, Nadine. She's made a lot of progress. And if she overheard ya talkin' like that, it might push her off the wagon again,"

"Are you still worried she's gonna go back to drinkin'?"

"Sometimes. I guess that's why I've been tryin' so hard to behave and help around here."

"She isn't your responsibility, Jane. She never was," Nadine said angrily.

"Well, if I hadn't picked her head up outta the toilet all them times, then she wouldn't be here, 'cause she would've drowned in her own vomit.

"Okay, okay! Stop trippin', Jane. How did we get so far off the track?"

"Sorry, Nadine. I guess I still have some worries about her goin' back to her old ways. I'm still worried that problems will come up even here that will upset her to the point that she wants to drink again."

"She isn't going to, Jane. Dad takes her to them meetin's every week, and she's gonna make it. Stop worryin' about makin' her mad. She ain't hit you even once since she's been back."

It felt good to confide my fears in Nadine. I knew that she understood me more than anyone could, and it was a huge relief to be able to voice my concerns out loud instead of holding it all in. Still, I felt the need to do as Mitchell had said regarding Elijah. Maybe he knew something that I didn't, I wasn't sure, but I didn't want to cause anything to go awry in this new house of harmony.

"So are ya gonna tell me what happened with Benjamin?"

"He asked me to court him again, but I asked him for more time to think, and he consented. Now, I have to come up with the right answer."

"Nadine, why don't you just put it out of your mind until you know for sure how you feel about him," I suggested.

"Well, I already like him a lot, and I suppose it wouldn't hurt to accept his courting proposal, but I don't have the guts to ask dad."

"Pretty soon ya won't have to. After your birthday, it won't be an issue. After all, it was dad himself that said ya could court when ya turned seventeen."

"Thanks for remindin' me of that fact. It'll come in handy when I'm breakin' the news to them."

"Does that mean what I think it means, Nadine?"

"Yeah, I think I just made up my mind," she said with a smile.

We both let out a squeal, then, hushed each other, not wanting anyone else in the house to hear.

ෂංඥ

After my talk with Nadine, I felt more inspired than ever to help Hannah. Making a friend and learning new skills such as shucking corn and shelling peas felt like an easy way to start learning more about the Amish ways that would come in handy if I decided to join them as my brother and sister had chosen to do. I knew it wasn't an easy decision for Nadine to make, but I admired her for making up her mind; something I wondered if I would have the guts to do if and when the opportunity presented itself.

ตดตช

The leaves began to turn beautiful hues of red and yellow due to early frosts. Rain, it seemed, would wait awhile, leaving us with eighty-degree days. The warmth of the Indian summer was enjoyable to me but, most of all, pleasing to the local farmers who still had a great deal of harvesting to tend to.

In spite of harvest season being in full swing, Elijah and Benjamin continued to take Nadine and me to school every morning, long after my ankle had healed. They weren't always able to pick us up at the end of the school day, though. In between working their own land, they were still busy coaching Mitchell on his farming skills, so he would be able to provide for Rebekah once the two of them wed.

On Saturday, after the noon meal, neighbor women gathered at the Zook's house to prepare the wedding ring patterned quilt to add to Rebekah's wedding dowry. We had all been busy making tea towels and hand-stitched linens for her as well. Elijah's *mam* was a great instructor and she was very patient in teaching us how to sew and crochet.

As I watched Rebekah gracefully arrange the fabric swatches, I wondered if my brother knew how fortunate he was to have such a wonderful woman love him. If she had met him even a few short years before, she might have run the other way because of his bitterness. She truly loved him, and his past attitudes were no longer important because they had all been forgiven and remained in the past.

୧୦ଔ

Hannah Lapp was the first in attendance for the quilting, with her *mam*, Martha. Rachel Miller, and her two daughters, Miriam and Abigail, brought some beautiful patchwork squares that were left over from Abigail's quilting. The Miller sisters, Mary, Elizabeth and Leah, who had lost their *mam*, were also in attendance for their cousin. Even Deborah Yoder and her sister, Lydia, made the effort to come, along with their *mam*, Sarah.

I was surprised to see Deborah at the quilting, after the argument she and Nadine had over Benjamin Lapp. Nadine had won that disagreement, and in the end, made the right decision, as far as I was concerned. My father had been much obliged to give his permission for the two to begin courting after Nadine's birthday. Nadine was pleased when our parents presented her with a cedar chest packed with things for her own dowry. She also received a silver locket, into which she promptly placed a lock of Benjamin's hair. I was excited for Nadine, but it made me anxious to court Elijah, even though he hadn't officially asked me yet. Our biggest obstacle would be getting past my father before my seventeenth birthday—I wasn't sure I could wait another entire year.

In two days, Elijah and I would celebrate our birthday together and I had never been more aflame with excitement. I was secretly hoping my father would allow more than friendship for the two of us, after giving permission to Nadine and Benjamin to begin courting. I was also counting on Mitchell's upcoming wedding in November to be helpful in bringing the families together more often.

ഗരു

At the quilting, the women began their stitching— and their stories. Gossip was more like it, but I held my tongue. I was shocked that Amish women gossiped, but I kept out of it. I suppose I hadn't realized before now that everyone is susceptible to the "gossip bug", but I didn't want to be any part of the talk. I was too busy thinking about how much I wanted to sneak out and spend some time with Elijah. I sure was tired of the women and their talking by the end of the evening. Though the quilting went smoothly enough, we would need to gather together two more nights to complete the already beautiful quilt. Just when I started to get the hang of it, the quilting bee was over, and my sore fingertips told me it was for the best.

At four o'clock, the women left to prepare the evening meal at their own homes. I decided that helping my mother in the kitchen would be the perfect opportunity to pitch my ideas about my birthday. I made small talk about Nadine's and Rebekah's dowries, hoping it would lead to talk of courting.

Instead, we worked in silence for the most part. We put away the leftover cakes and refreshments and washed the teacups. I tried hard to steer the nearly one-sided conversation toward the subject of my birthday with Elijah, but it seemed that my mother was too wrapped up in Mitchell's wedding plans to pay attention to my constant chatter.

Dad poked his head in the doorway to the kitchen and interrupted me just as I got up enough nerve to ask outright about my birthday plans.

"How about we spend a little quality family time together tonight," he said.

"Go ahead, Jane, I'll finish up in here. As soon as I get the rest of these teacups put in the cupboard, I'll be in there to help you, Jack," my mother said.

"Don't take too long, you'll miss all the good stuff," he said as he kissed her on the cheek.

My mother giggled—something I was still getting used to hearing from her. My father smiled at her as though to say he was very much in love with her. I enjoyed seeing my parents act that way, after hearing nothing but fighting between them only a few months before.

⁊

As our game of charades neared its end, Daniel Zook rushed in through the side door trying to speak, though he was out of breath. My father initially became a little annoyed with him, thinking he'd come to play with Cameron.

"Aunt Naomi needs ya quick," he managed to say to my mother. "The babies are coming too fast, and she's asking for ya, Mrs. Reeves."

Nadine gestured for the two of us to go—she would put the younger children to bed. Normally I would jump at any opportunity to be at Elijah's house, but the thought of being in the same house with someone who was giving birth made me feel uneasy.

We each grabbed a sweater before walking out into the cool, night air. I held my mother's arm as we walked as swiftly as she was able across the property. Daniel pushed down the broken boards of the fence so my mother and I could cross over safely.

"I'll have to remember to thank Abraham for not repairing the fence right away," my mother said lightly. "I don't think this baby I'm carrying would have allowed me to get all the way down our driveway and back up theirs without having to use the outhouse."

"Uncle Abe told me that having a gate right here was overdue," Daniel said.

"Well that sounds like a fine idea," My mother agreed.

I had to admit, I wasn't looking forward to an evening of running to the Zook's outhouse myself. As far as I was concerned, hopping over the fence to use our toilet was just as quick as using the outhouse at the back of the Zook's yard.

The closer we got to their farm, the more clearly we could hear the cries that were coming from inside the house. When we entered the Zook's kitchen, Abraham was pacing the floors with a look of deep anguish on his face. I could see the distress in the lines of his face as he beckoned my mother into the room where Naomi was moaning.

"Rebekah is in there with her. Elijah and Samuel went for the midwife," he said.

He then ushered my mother toward the bedroom that was on the main level of the house, off to the side of the kitchen. I offered to walk Rachel over to my house to be with Lucy so she would be out of earshot of her mother's moaning and groaning. Mr. Zook agreed.

ಬೂಲಣ

Back over the fence I went, this time with Rachel in tow. I was grateful for the walk back to my house so I'd be able to use the bathroom before returning to the Zook's, since the chilly air was making me feel uncomfortable.

As we walked the length of the property, the drying grass crunched somewhat under our feet. Neither of us said a word, but our footsteps drowned out the faint, cringing sounds that were still audible even at this distance.

Did Mamma go through that every time she gave birth to each of us? Maybe I don't want any kids after all, if it hurts that much.

Once inside my own home, I used the modern bathroom and hurried back over to the Zook's. I entered their yard in time to see Elijah and Samuel ride up to the house with Mary Beiler, the midwife. She rode a much smaller horse, but being a woman, I thought that it suited her.

Elijah spotted me and jumped off Eli, allowing Samuel to take him into the barn. He led the other two horses with him by their reigns. Elijah walked over to me and took both my hands in his.

"I'm so glad you're here for this wonderful miracle," he said

I shook at the thought of returning to the Zook's kitchen and being within earshot of Naomi's cries, even though I hadn't heard any for several minutes. Elijah seemed to sense my reluctance and my fear, for he drew me close to him and held me gently in his arms.

"Did *Mam's* screams worry you?" he asked.

It was a fair question, and certainly one that deserved an answer, but I wasn't able to think clearly at the moment. I was too afraid that if I spoke, he would let go of his grasp on me. In the stillness of the evening, I could hear my own heart beating to the gentle rhythm of the cricket's song. I rested my head on his broad shoulder, allowing him to comfort me.

Without warning, Samuel came running from the barn and startled me enough to make me back away from Elijah. I didn't look at Samuel or Elijah due to the worry I felt from getting caught in a position that I knew I shouldn't be in.

After Samuel ran into the house, Elijah put his hands on my shoulders but I couldn't face him.

"Don't worry about Samuel, he won't tell anyone what he saw. Brothers are loyal to one another," Elijah whispered quietly in my ear.

"I'm sure he won't, but that could have been my daddy seein' us," I whispered.

I wanted to be back in his arms, but I knew I shouldn't. I somehow gained enough strength to turn around and usher Elijah back into the house. I was glad we did because Abraham walked out onto the porch as we approached it, and I feared he could have caught us holding one another if we hadn't walked toward the house when we did.

Elijah and I sat at the long table inside the kitchen, while Abraham remained out on the porch in plain view. I quickly scanned the room, making sure we were alone before speaking to Elijah about what was suddenly weighing heavily on my mind.

"Why doesn't your papa stay in the room with your *mam*? And why do they use a midwife instead of Doctor Beiler? " I asked quietly. Though we were alone, I still felt it best to whisper.

"That's just his way," he whispered just as I had. "The midwife is Doc Beiler's wife and she's been there for the birth of each of us children."

I didn't understand, given the fact that my parents had always been together at a hospital during each of our births. My father had never left my mamma's side when each of us children was born—not even for a minute. I wondered if she would use the midwife for the birth of the baby she was carrying now since we came to live in this community. My thoughts were draining and I was eager to leave the Zook's home.

Suddenly, my distressing thoughts were interrupted by the sharp cry of a baby, coming from the room where Naomi was giving birth. Elijah and I looked at each other with excitement, then, listened for the other baby to cry, but it didn't. The color drained from my face as I heard a shrill cry from Naomi. Elijah held my hand tight as we held our breath in anticipation for the other cry to come, but still, it didn't. I couldn't take being within earshot of Naomi's cries anymore. In my fear, I stood to leave the house, when I finally heard a second cry.

"Was that the other baby? Please, Elijah tell me it was," I whispered, through quivering lips.

Before he could answer, Rebekah opened the door with a weary look on her face. She beckoned us in and called for Abraham before going back in the room. Elijah pushed open the screen-door to alert his father it was time to come in the house. I stood aside to let Abraham and Elijah go first, then, I craned my head around the door of the dimly lit room, unsure of what I would find on the other side. At the foot of the bed, my mother and Rebekah were each washing a baby girl as the midwife tended to Mrs. Zook, urging her to drink some hot cider. The flickering of the lanterns cast shadows on Mrs. Zook, enhancing her Plain beauty.

Seeing the twins and hearing their cries caused my heart to flutter. Elijah reached over and squeezed my hand, while I allowed tears to fall unchecked from my eyes at the beautiful sight before me. Abraham led us in a prayer of thanks as we bowed our heads in reverence for such a joyous miracle.

At my mother's signal, Elijah and I left the room. I was fully prepared to wait for her to finish so I could escort her home. Elijah and I decided to get Rachel from my house in the meantime, so she could meet her new baby sisters. She didn't need to be convinced, for she ran ahead of us in her excitement. Neither of us cared to keep up with her, so we lingered between the two properties, waiting for my mother to exit the Zook's back door.

"I have to admit I was a little scared back there before we saw both babies in the room," he said with a sigh.

I faced him, looking into his blue eyes, and wondering about his deep compassion for his family.

"Have you and your family always been so close?" I asked with hesitation.

I knew I was opening the door to a conversation I wasn't sure I was ready to trust Elijah with yet, but I knew he cared enough about me not to judge my past.

"We were raised to be supportive of one another. Weren't you?"

"Up until a couple of months back, our family was a mess, but it's been gettin' better every day since," I explained.

"I'm sorry that ya had such a tough time, but what's important is that ya have your family now."

His smile enticed an equal one from me. It was easy to smile in his presence because he made me feel so accepted. His friendship was truly unconditional and I longed to be able to return the same to him, but unconditional love didn't come as naturally to me as it seemed to for him.

"Will ya tell me about your childhood—someday when you're ready?" he asked slowly.

"Someday," I said.

I only said it to humor him, but somehow, deep down, he seemed like the one that I might someday trust to share my entire life story with. Not any time soon, though, I was certain.

We stood hand in hand, relaying unspoken messages through our deep gaze into each other's eyes.

"What shall we do for our birthday? A picnic on the creek bank, maybe?" he asked, changing the subject.

"A picnic would be wonderful but I'm afraid I don't have a gift for ya," I said with dismay.

"Ya don't need to give me anything; your company is enough to make it a happy birthday for me."

He smiled enough to show his dimples, and I smiled out of the love that rested in my heart for him.

The squeak of the screen door brought me back to reality as my mother walked out onto the back porch of the Zook's home.

"I'm over here," I called to her. I held up a hand and waved her toward where Elijah and I had been standing for some time. Elijah and I assisted the worn out woman back to her own porch, then embraced each other briefly after she went in. His cheek brushed against mine as he whispered in my ear to have a *gut* night. The sensation of his lips against my ear nearly made me lose my train of thought. I wanted so much to have his lips touch mine, but I was glad he didn't attempt such a thing just yet because I was sure I wasn't quite ready to handle it as a proper lady should. I walked into the house feeling as though I were truly in love. Common sense reminded me that I'd only known him for a short time, and it was too soon to tell if it was really love. My heart, however, raced with excitement over the thought of this boy who would soon be a man— perhaps the man I might want to marry—someday.

FIVE
A TIME TO COURT

Early the next morning, I was up and ready for church before anyone else in the house. Our rooster crowed a little earlier than usual, relieving me from my restlessness. After the excitement of the twins' birth last night, I was eager to see Elijah again.

A knock at the side door startled me just as I finished ironing the wrinkles from the white apron for my Sunday dress. I wasn't surprised to see Elijah when I went to the door, but I momentarily panicked, thinking something may be wrong.

"Is everything okay with your *mam* and the twins?"

"They were up for the better part of the night, but they are resting now."

"Whew!" I said, wiping the back of my hand across my forehead dramatically. "Ya had me worried there for a minute."

"Will ya come out side and talk to me for a minute? I have something to ask you."

Elijah turned off the generator that temporarily powered the laundry room as I walked out the side door while tying my apron.

"I sure will be glad when the windmill gets put up so I won't have to use that generator any more—it's so loud. I know my father has his heart set on getting electricity to this old farmhouse."

"Ya don't have any idea how pleased my papa was by his decision to use the windmill instead of having the county hook up modern electricity. Not to mention the money your papa saved by doing it this way."

"I suppose you're right—I just need to learn more patience, I guess. So, what did ya wanna talk to me about, Elijah?"

"I know it's early, but I had to see ya. Do ya think you could get permission to go to the Singing tonight?"

"There is no way that my daddy is gonna let me go. This'll be Nadine's first time. He wouldn't even let her go 'till she had her birthday," I said around the lump that was forming in my throat.

"Couldn't ya just go with Hannah and Nadine?"

"Hannah is going?"

I sounded whiney and desperate like Nadine.

"Don't be upset because she's going."

I tried calming down, but found myself tapping my foot and pursing my lips in anger instead.

"Hannah has gone a few times," he finally said. "Benjamin told me that she would go with you tonight if it would help convince your papa."

"I don't think I even want to ask. When he says 'no', I'll get even more upset."

I meant what I said and he didn't press any further. He lingered impatiently, holding my hand. I couldn't look up at him for fear that tears might spill from my watery eyes. He kissed the back of my hand softly and I knew it was his subtle way of preparing for his exit.

"Well, I should get back to my chores or I'll never be ready for church."

He kissed my cheek and walked off toward his barn, leaving me with feelings of excitement over the kiss, mixed with anguish over not being able to attend the Singing. It was already starting to feel like a very long day and the sun was just beginning to make its way over the rolling hills that seemed to stretch across unending miles of earth.

ॐ

Inside the church, the Mennonite families sat together, as did our family. Many of the Amish families, however, sat in Old Order fashion, with the men on one side and the women on the other. Most of the Amish families that attended, used the last rows in the church, which I thought made it seem almost segregated, but my father said they did it out of respect to the Mennonites since it was their church. The minister offered words of wisdom to the congregation, but my mind was not on his teaching— it was cluttered with worries of my earlier conversation with Elijah. I knew it was wrong to think such selfish thoughts in church, but no matter how much I tried, I just couldn't keep from thinking about Elijah. I periodically looked back at him where he sat with his brother and cousins.

After church services, I overheard Mamma offering to take a meal over to the Zook's so Naomi could get her much-needed bed rest. Rebekah assured her that she could keep things under control until her *mam* was on her feet again. She did, however, graciously accept the apple pies that my mother had baked the day before.

When we reached home, I was asked to take the pies over to them and I gladly agreed. I hadn't had the opportunity to speak with Elijah since the morning, even though we spent a fair amount of time in church eyeing one another. I had a hard time enjoying the game of eye contact with him since Nadine nudged me a few times and warned me I was going straight to Hell if I didn't watch what I was thinking in church since God was able to read my thoughts. Her comments angered me, but I had to wonder if there was some truth to the seemingly logical statements.

After church, I was anxious to talk to Elijah to find out whether he was planning on attending the Sunday Singing, but I dreaded the thought that his answer would not be in my favor. Rachel opened the door when I knocked, took the pies and informed me that Elijah was in the barn, "In a bad mood," she said.

I walked slowly, trying to gather my thoughts before approaching him.

I hope he's not in a bad mood because of me. Maybe I should sneak out and go with Hannah. She's the same age as I am, and it ain't fair that she's goin' and I can't. It's not fair. It just isn't fair.

Tears welled up in my eyes, and before I knew it, I came face to face with Elijah.

"What's the matter, Jane?"

Elijah embraced me lightly but I pushed him away.

"Don't be mad at me, please don't be mad at me," I begged him. "I'll sneak out of the house if ya want me to go to the Singin' that bad."

I was practically crying by this time.

"Whoa, who said I was mad at ya?"

"Rachel said that you were in a bad mood."

"That doesn't mean I'm mad at you," he said softly. "I'm just disappointed that we can't go to the Singing, but I would never go without ya. And I would never ask ya to sneak out and defy your papa like that. That wouldn't be such a *gut* thing. Then I'd never get the chance to court ya proper-like."

"I'm sorry. I didn't mean to jump to conclusions. I wanna see ya so badly t'night," I said.

"Can ya stay for a while? I have chores, but I can talk while I work."

"I should get back. My mamma needs me to watch Molly while she prepares the evening meal."

He offered a friendly hug, then, whispered in my ear.

"At least they're letting ya stay home from school tomorrow for your birthday," he said cheerfully.

"It's not like I'm learnin' anything anyway. I wish my parents would either let me go to the public school or let me stay home," I said.

"Let's put all our worries behind us and think of our day tomorrow. I'm looking forward to our day together."

"You're right. I'm looking forward to our picnic, too."

He kissed me on my forehead, then told me to go before someone came looking for me. I left reluctantly but happier than when I'd first seen him.

Despite the fact that Elijah and I would remain home from the Singing, I still continued to sulk the rest of the day. At dinner, I pushed my food around my plate so much that my mother asked me to leave the table.

Mitchell followed me outside. "What's on yer mind squirt?"

"Stop talking to me like I'm a child, Mitchell. That's all anyone does anymore. I'm not a child. I'm growing up."

He sat on the porch swing beside me and began to push with one foot. "Everyone can see how much yer growin' up. Why do ya think the folks want to keep you down a bit?"

He didn't give me a chance to answer.

"It's so ya don't grow up *too* fast."

"But I'm tired of being treated like a little kid. And I'm upset because I don't have a birthday present for Elijah. I just feel like nothin' is gonna go right tomorrow."

Mitchell grabbed my hand and pulled me off the porch swing. "Come with me. I have an idea. Something that might make things a little better."

I followed him to the *Dawdi Haus* where he dug through a few boxes at the far end of the enclosed porch until he pulled what he was looking for from the last box.

"This is brand new. Still has the tags on it. I bought it just before we moved here thinking I would wear it, but all I wear is dirty jeans to work in the fields. Elijah is about the same size as I am. I think it'll fit him."

I took the tan, suede vest, feeling unsure of whether I should thank him or toss it aside.

"What's wrong?"

"It's not that I don't appreciate it, but what if Elijah doesn't like it? I've never seen any of the Amish boys wearing stuff like this."

"Even if he doesn't like it, he will like it just 'cause it's from you."

"That makes no sense at all but I hope yer right."

"Guys love getting gifts from girls. Trust me."

He took it back from me and cut the tags off.

"Now it'll look like it wasn't store-bought."

"Thanks Mitchell."

I left the porch of the *Dawdi Haus* feeling a lot better than I had at the dinner table. I'd have to remember to apologize to my mother for not eating the dinner she prepared.

ೞಞ

When the time came for Nadine to leave, I felt bitterness and jealousy rise up in me again. Hannah came to the door to alert Nadine that the group was ready to go. I forced a smile and told them both how wonderful they looked, but inside I was furious that I was being left out. After they left, I ran sobbing to my room and sat in the window seat, watching the horse-drawn buggies as they pulled away from the house.

I wasn't surprised to see Mitchell in the front seat of a buggy. He would be doing the driving for the evening. Mr. Zook still wasn't comfortable with Rebekah riding in our Volkswagen Bus *or* the station wagon so Mitchell often took her in Samuel Beiler's old courting buggy. Samuel had outgrown it since his marriage to Abigail Miller. His brother, Matthew, hadn't found anyone that interested him enough to court yet, so he was happy to loan it to Mitchell for the time being.

Benjamin drove his own courting buggy with Nadine in front with him, while Hannah rode in the back. I could hear them laughing as they left the long drive before turning onto the main road.

Too upset to bother with lighting the lantern, I wandered around my room with only the moonlight to guide me. Finding my long linen nightgown, I pulled it over my head and tied the ribbon at the ruffled neckline. Tears dropped from my eyes as I fidgeted with the ruffles that fell along my wrists. Curious thoughts filled my head causing me to wonder why I had acted like the child I was trying so desperately to leave behind. It felt awkward to have adult feelings and still be considered a child by all those around me. I wanted so much to be grown up.

Without warning, a light flashed from outside through the bedroom window several times. I sat still for a moment watching what seemed to be a pattern of flashes. Unsure of what it might be, I was cautious in going toward the window. Deciding it would be better to keep my distance, I stood on Nadine's bed in order to be high enough to see what was down below. A light shone on Elijah's face and I laughed aloud as I hopped from the bed to the floor. I pushed open the window and called out to him as quietly as I could.

"What're ya doin' here?"

I turned my head sideways and pressed my ear to the screen, thinking it would help me to hear his response.

"I came to rescue my fair maiden. Come down to meet your knight!"

"What do you know about fair maidens and knights?"

"I can read ya know."

He sounded insulted, but I giggled for a moment at his silliness, then, told him to wait while I looked for my robe. I struggled in the dark, only able to find my plaid poncho.

Deciding I would rather not use the poncho, I grabbed the cream-colored, tasseled throw blanket from the end of my bed and threw it about my shoulders. I rushed down the back stairs and crept out the side door beneath my bedroom window. His arms reached out to me and I went to him without hesitation. I could have let him hold me all night except for the fact that I was curious to find out why he had really come to see me.

"What're ya doin' here? I felt so left out when everyone went to the Singin'. Oh, it doesn't matter, I'm just so glad you're here."

I flung myself back in his arms, not wanting him to let go.

"I told you I wouldn't go to the Singing without you. You're my fair maiden."

We both laughed heartily, then, hushed each other so we wouldn't be heard.

"Let's go over and sit under the tree," he suggested.

"So how did ya know which window was mine?" I asked, pointing upward.

"I have a little confession of my own," he said, covering his face momentarily. "When ya first moved in, I would often see ya sitting in the window and I'd watch you. All the while, I wondered who ya were and what could possibly have made you so sad."

"I love that window seat. It was the only thing that made my movin' here a little easier. I suppose it's because it became my new thinkin' spot."

"Every time I'd see ya sitting there, I would wonder how long it would be before I could meet you. I would sit and watch ya twisting your beautiful wavy hair between your fingers, wondering if I would ever be able to touch it."

He reached out and grabbed a curl that hung alongside of my face and twisted it the way I always did. He smiled mischievously, causing me to feel suddenly very shy.

We sat under the large maple tree, and talked for nearly two hours. When we began to hear the gentle clip-clop of the horse's hooves, we knew that the courtiers were coming home. Elijah helped me to my feet, pulled me close and kissed me square on the lips, then, left me at the back porch. I was too much in shock from the kiss to go back in the house just then, so I waited a while, allowing the gentle rhythm of the cricket's song to trap me in a mesmerized state just a little while longer.

ಬಂಧ

In the morning, I was too excited about my birthday to stay in bed. Being a Monday, my father had to work so I wanted to catch him before he left. Thinking back on previous birthdays made me appreciate this one the most. I realized that this birthday would mark the first year I wouldn't have to solicit well wishes from my family. Today, I determined, would be the most special of all birthdays ever because I would spend it with Elijah, whom I genuinely loved.

The smell of fresh coffee made its way up the stairs as I pulled my robe from the peg behind my bedroom door. After brushing my teeth, I crept down the stairs so as not to wake my mother. Before reaching the bottom of the stairwell, I overheard voices and decided it was best not to enter the room just yet. Strangely, my mother was up, and having what sounded to me to be a serious conversation with my father. I decided to sit in the front room to allow them some private time before I interrupted. My ears perked up when I heard Elijah's name mentioned. "But Anna, she's clearly attached to the boy already and I'm sure his intentions are proper. Elijah ain't lookin' to get her into trouble," my father said.

Get me in trouble how? What're they talkin' about?
Before I had much time to think about it, the
question was answered for me.

"Since our talk with Abraham and Naomi, the two
of them have gotten a little more chummy," my mother was
saying.

We're not chums. We're much more than that.

The thought of my parents having a talk with the
Zook's about Elijah and me was enough to make my
stomach turn. It made me nervous—even a little angry.

"After the party tonight, the four of us should sit
down and have a talk with the two of them. If they intend to
court, they'll need some talkin' to so we can set things
straight with them," my father finished.

He kissed my mother, and was out the door before I
had time to think about losing my chance to talk to him. I
crept back up the stairs, figuring it was better that I not let
on that I'd eavesdropped on a conversation that I shouldn't
have. Then I knelt down beside my bed to whisper a prayer.

"God, if you're there, I beg of ya to take away the
nervous feelin' in my stomach. I'm worried that Mamma
and Daddy will never let me court Elijah. Ya know how
much I love him already and I know he loves me too, even
if he hasn't admitted it yet. Please help me. Bless us on our
birthday today, and let Elijah like the gift I'm givin' him.
Ya know I ain't got any real bread to buy him somethin'
cool, unless ya count what's in my piggy-bank. I know it
don't matter to Elijah if I buy him somethin'. I'm not
complainin', God, but I wish I had more cash to get him
somethin' nicer. I know Mitchell said he'd like the vest, but
he ain't Amish, so he don't know for sure what Elijah
would like or not. Thanks for all your blessin's, and thanks

for making Mitchell so generous and givin' me the vest so I could give it to Elijah. Amen."

Nadine stirred in her bed a little, so I decided it was best if I left the room to shower. When I returned from the bathroom, Nadine was sitting up on her bed, looking as though she were thinking earnestly.

"Is anything wrong, Nadine," I asked her quietly.

"No, it's just that I heard ya prayin' and I know ya don't know if Elijah will like your gift or not. I wasn't eavesdroppin', I just sorta overheard ya. I'm pretty sure he'll like it just 'cause it's from you."

I sat there, bewildered for a moment, unable to process her statement.

"Yeah, that's what Mitchell said. Don't worry about it. I think it's a hopeless cause," I finally said.

"Try to think of a backup plan; somethin' he likes to do or anything he might have said that would be pleasin' to him. Might there have been anything he's been hinting' to ya about?"

She took her time asking the question, as though she were also giving it some thought. Suddenly, the most wonderful idea came to my head. I was so elated that I hopped over to Nadine and gave her a squeeze around her shoulders.

"Oh! Wait—never mind."

I slumped back down on my own bed.

"I had a great idea, but I just realized that I have no idea how to go about it. There's no way that I can do the only thing that Elijah has told me he would like."

I sulked as I pulled my knees to my chest and leaned up against the wall that my bed bordered. When I finally looked over at Nadine, she seemed to have a confused look on her face. I reached over and waved my hand in front her face to get her attention but it did no good. She jumped when I tapped her arm, which made me jump back a little.

This started us laughing, though we immediately began shushing each other to keep from waking Rachel who lay undisturbed in her bed on the other side of the room.

"What was yer idea, and why is it impossible?"

I sat down on her bed to explain my plan and how I didn't know how to fix my hair the way that Elijah had suggested.

"Is that all?"

I was a little offended that she had taken my dilemma so lightly.

"What do ya mean, 'is that all'," I snapped at her. "This is a big deal to me, I'm sixteen now—almost a woman!"

I could see that Nadine was suppressing a smile, which caused me to laugh at myself. She joined in and we started shushing one another again.

"I'll help ya. We can get Mom's bobby pins and her Aqua Net to tack it down so the top won't move around."

"Fine, but Elijah said he'd like it if I left a few curls to dangle around my face, like this," I tried demonstrating to her.

"Ooh. That's gonna look awful pretty."

After getting permission from my mother to use her things for my experimental "grown-up" hairstyle, we set to work on various ways to accomplish the task at hand. First it was too high on my head, then, the next few tries ended up falling out. I began to get a little flustered at the several failed attempts.

"Maybe this was a stupid idea," I said. "I'll just go with my hair down like I always do."

I pouted some more, thinking it would make me feel better, but it didn't.

"Why are you giving up, Jane?"

"Because I'm never going to get it to look the way Elijah wanted it."

Nadine rolled her eyes. "I don't know why you have to be so perfect for him."

"Because I really like him a lot and I want him to be attracted to me too."

Nadine shook her head. "I get positive vibes when he's around you. He obviously thinks you're cool or he wouldn't want to spend his birthday with ya, Jane. He would've blown you off."

I pursed my lips. "I don't want him to think I'm cool. I want him to fall in love with me."

My heart skipped a beat when my mother suddenly appeared behind me. We caught each other's eye in the bathroom mirror, and I wondered how much of the conversation she had heard between Nadine and me.

"Would you like some help?"

My mother's voice was quiet and controlled.

"We can't seem to get my dumb hair to go the right way," I answered nervously.

She moved between us and began twisting and turning my hair in several directions before she started pinning it in place. I kept my head down out of fear that it still wouldn't be what I'd pictured it in my head. After feeling a few more sticks and pinches on my head from the pins, I slowly opened my eyes to view the finished product. At first, I was stunned. I stared for a long time, turning my head every which way to see it from every angle.

"Do you think this is what Elijah had in mind?" my mother asked, a smile forming crinkles at the corners of her eyes.

Most of the color drained from my face, because at that moment I knew she had heard me speak of Elijah. I pulled once or twice at the wavy strands of hair that were determined to hang in my face; as if I needed another distraction today.

"Mamma. I uh, uh."

It was no use. I was cornered and couldn't talk my way out of this one no matter how hard I tried. I'd never been quick witted—that was Nadine's talent.

"Don't worry; I know how special he is to you. I think he's a very good friend for you," she said.

A good friend? I wanted him for more than a friend. I was in love with him.

The color returned to my cheeks, making me look as embarrassed as I felt because I knew I wanted more than friendship from Elijah.

Just when I thought my mother was going to leave the room, she reached around the back of the bathroom door and lifted something on a hanger from the doorknob.

"Surprise!"

She was beaming and I was speechless as she presented me with a long-sleeved dress of pale blue, with creamy white embroidery on the sleeves. The white ruffle on the collar of the dress was delicately embroidered to match the sleeves. The length was shorter, at calf-length, making it less formal than some of the dresses I wore to church.

"Oh, this is wonderful!"

"I'm glad you like it, Jane."

"Oh, but is it too fancy? All the Amish girls wear white or black aprons with solid colored dresses. Hannah's the only one that I've seen wearing a calico, and this isn't even calico—it's very different."

"This will look beautiful with your hairstyle. And don't worry about it being too fancy—Elijah's *mam* helped me to choose the material at Fork's General Store. I'm certain Elijah won't find it too fancy either," my mother said.

I hugged her excitedly, but her kindness confused me a little. It was strange having her as a mother again. For several years, I had taken care of her—and now, she was taking care of me—and I liked it.

I studied her for just a moment.

My mother was really a very beautiful woman—not just on the outside anymore. Her eyes no longer carried anger in them. I could almost see a hint of chocolate in her brown eyes that smiled with contentment. Her long, auburn hair was pulled up neatly in the front exposing rosy cheeks where dullness used to dominate her face. She looked younger and happier than I'd seen her in a very long time; and that made me smile.

೫໐ఴ

The noon hour finally arrived and it was a good thing because I had all but worn a path in the wooden floor of my room. I grabbed the suede vest that Mitchell had given me, suddenly wondering if I should leave it behind and show up without a gift. Instead, I had a sudden idea, and pushed open my jewelry box, removing my silver peace-sign necklace with the brown, leather lanyard and shoved it in my apron pocket. After pacing for nearly twenty minutes in my room, I stole a final glance in the bathroom mirror and headed down the stairs on shaky legs. Why am I so nervous? I can do this. I've spent a lot of time with Elijah. This time is no different. Yes it is. Who am I kidding? What if he kisses me? I guess I'll have to just kiss him back.

The clip-clop of Eli's hooves sent my heart fluttering. My hand shook as I reached for the door handle. I paused for a minute to gain some control over my emotions, but no matter how hard I tried, I couldn't seem to force my hand to turn the handle. When a knock came at the door, I nearly lost my breath with the heavy gasp that escaped my lips.

The door opened and Elijah poked his head in. I didn't move from my spot until he caught sight of me cowering behind the door. The look on his face, and the mist in his eyes made me want him to sweep me into his arms. Instead, he offered his arm to escort me out to his waiting horse.

Before boosting me up on Eli, he pulled his other hand out from behind his back to reveal the bouquet of wild flowers he had picked for me that were tied together with a yellow ribbon. I recognized them as the same flowers from the trail beside his field.

"Wild flowers for my little wild flower," he said as he handed them to me.

"Thank you," I whispered.

The bouquet was full of multi-colored cosmos, daisies and black-eyed Susans, which were all my favorite flowers

Elijah assisted me in mounting side-saddle on the horse that had a blanket draped over the saddle. He scanned the area for onlookers, then, settled in his usual spot behind me on Eli. After we were a safe distance into the thick of the trees away from my house, he gave me a quick squeeze and nuzzled his face in my neck to whisper in my ear.

"Blue is definitely your color, and your hair is beautiful up. Thank you for such a wonderful surprise."

Mission accomplished. He likes my dress *and* my hair.

I felt so beautiful.

I kept my thoughts to myself and just smiled. Nadine told me that Elijah would not like me if I was vain. He didn't even know we had mirrors in our house. My father told us the Amish see vanity as a sin and won't hang mirrors in their homes. It was my opinion that everyone should be able to enjoy seeing how God made them, but Nadine would probably say that way of thinking was a sin in their eyes, too.

With a click from Elijah's heel, the horse walked slowly toward the creek. When we reached the special spot we'd planned for our picnic, he halted the horse but made no advance toward dismounting. I suddenly felt the shock of the gentle sweeping of his mouth across the back of my neck and close to my ear, and realized he was kissing me softly. It was both scary and wonderful at the same time.

My first instinct was that anything this wonderful had to be wrong. Second thoughts allowed me the luxury of being held by the one I loved and experiencing my first passionate kiss. I contemplated turning my head to kiss his lips but decided against it. These thoughts caused me to become rigid enough to signal to Elijah to cease his actions. He stopped kissing my neck and held me close to him. Being in his arms felt so natural, I couldn't imagine being anywhere else at the moment. He hopped down from the horse, and held my hand while I slid gracefully toward the ground.

Once my feet touched the ground, I stood facing Elijah.

Neither of us spoke.

He was somehow holding both my hands and used them to draw me to him. I felt soft lips touch mine, as my eyes closed.

The kiss was unexpectedly long, and passionate.

"Happy birthday," he whispered, allowing the corners of his mouth to give way to a full grin.

The kissing continued, and would have gone on forever had I not gathered my wits about me. I pulled slightly away, giving him the message that the all-too-wonderful kiss was over for now.

"Shall we eat?" he asked awkwardly.

"I'll spread the blanket near the slope of the crick bank," I offered, as he grabbed the leather satchel containing our food that was fastened to the saddle.

We both picked at our lunch, while making small talk. For some time, we steered clear of the subject of romance. But Elijah finally brought it to light—as though he just couldn't resist.

"Is it true what they say, about 'sweet sixteen—never been kissed'?"

He emanated a smile.

"Well, actually," I said slowly, "I'm afraid Bradley, a boy from Texas, has already beaten ya to it."

I laughed nervously, but he seemingly shrugged it off.

"I've never been kissed like that before—I mean, the way that you kissed me. Bradley's kiss was just a childhood crush; like puppy-love."

He took my hands in his and looked very seriously into my eyes.

"I don't care if this wasn't your first kiss. I love you, Jane."

"You do? I love you, too," I said. "With all my heart."

"May I call on you?"

"What?"

"I would like to court you, Jane."

"I'm not allowed to court 'till I'm seventeen."

I choked back tears while making this confession.

His blue eyes sparkled in the sun, inviting me to be nearer to him. I leaned over bravely and kissed him. He returned the kiss gently and lovingly, then, held me away from him.

"I will just have to ask your father for your hand," he said in between kisses.

"What do ya mean you'll ask my father for my hand?"

I was unsure of his declaration and I definitely needed to be clear on this account.

"I love you!" he said with a raised voice, then, his resonance quieted. "I want to marry ya some day. I have from the moment I laid eyes on your beautiful face—from the very first time I heard your sweet voice. I am committed to making ya happy for the rest of our lives."

I was too stunned to speak. Tears rolled down my face as I leapt into his arms.

After a few minutes, I faced him with a serious look on my face.

"Elijah, I want to marry you, too."

He held me close, kissing my neck and whispering how much he loved me in my ear.

After a few minutes, he stopped abruptly. "What's in the paper bag ya brought with you? Is it birthday cake?"

I leaned over and picked up the bag and set it in his lap.

"It's actually a gift for you."

His eyes widened with surprise, but I was nervous about what was in the bag, fearing he wouldn't like it. Before I could change my mind, he opened the bag and pulled out the vest. He unfolded it carefully, examining the stitch-work.

"This was made by hand. Did you make this yourself?"

I giggled slightly, remembering my conversation with my brother.

"No. Mitchell cut the tag out of it for me. He said it would make it look homemade."

He pulled his shirt from the waist of his trousers, then, began to unbutton each button slowly as I watched.

I felt my face heat up. "You can wear the vest over your shirt."

He ignored me and continued to unbutton his shirt. He smiled at me as he removed the shirt. I smiled back, though I could feel my cheeks burning with shyness. I knew I should have looked away, but I couldn't help but stare at his washboard stomach and slightly muscular chest.

"I saw a kid in town wearing a vest like this, but he wore it without a shirt. He also wore a necklace made of shells. How do I look?"

I pulled the "peace" necklace from my apron pocket and placed it around his neck.

"Now you don't look Amish anymore. You look like a hippie."

He pulled me close to him and kissed me like he never wanted to let me go, but he did finally.

"I have something for you, too."

He picked up the leather satchel and grabbed a clump of material from the bottom. When he held it up, I could see that it was a scarf for my hair. It was pale pastel stripes of color with tiny beads and bells that jingled from the fringe that hung from the ends.

"It's very pretty. Did you make this?"

"I wish I could say yes, but I purchased it at the flea market in Shipshewana."

"Help me unpin my hair so I can try it on."

Together, we pulled the bobby-pins from my hair. I combed through the hairspray-laden strands with my fingers to flatten it out, then, tied the scarf around the front.

I turned to Elijah. "How does it look?"

He put his hand to his chin as though he were studying me. "I think it's missing one thing."

He picked up the bouquet of flowers he'd given me and plucked a daisy from its stem, then, placed it carefully behind my ear.

"That's perfect. Now we both look like hippies."

"What do you know about hippies, Elijah?"

"I've seen them around town. I'm not blind."

We laughed and kissed again, then, leaned back on the blanket that was spread for our picnic. Since neither of us felt like eating any more, we remained quiet in each other's arms enjoying the late afternoon sun. I was in shock at how the day had turned out—certainly not how I had expected it to. I had to admit, I couldn't stop thinking about his proposal, or his bare chest. The only thing that was on my mind was how to break the news to my parents about the proposal, and how they would take it. My mother would probably smile, but sternly remind me of the rules, while my father would be very tough to convince.

When the sun began to blend into the horizon, we knew we had over-stayed our allotted time. I couldn't bring myself to leave until I was ready, and I wasn't sure I'd ever be ready to leave his side. I didn't readily care that I could risk being grounded for life by staying. Even then, it felt as though the time had traveled too fast, and it didn't seem fair. Elijah pulled a pocket watch from his trousers and showed me the time. It was nearing six o'clock, and we were expected at the family gathering for our birthday dinner. The reluctant look in his eyes as he put his shirt back on and placed the vest over the shirt made me feel sad.

Once we mounted the horse, Elijah gave me a squeeze and kissed my neck softly. We both understood it would need to last us until we could be alone again. Elijah allowed Eli to walk with a slow trot, making our ride home last a little longer than usual.

After the quiet ride, we left Eli in the Zook's barn and began to walk over to my house where everyone was waiting for us.

"Wait here. I forgot something."

Elijah ran across the length of the properties to his house. I waited on the steps for him, mostly because I didn't want to walk in late for dinner by myself. When he returned, he presented me with a package wrapped in plain brown paper with twine wrapped around it.

I placed a hand on the scarf on my head. "You already gave me a gift. What's this?"

"Just open it."

Inside the packaging was a hand-crocheted shawl of pale blue and creamy white. Elijah gently wrapped it around me, lifting the waves of hair we'd unpinned that had fallen across my shoulders. The colors matched my new dress perfectly. I found it tough to speak, but after a moment of admiring my gift, regained my countenance.

"Thank you so much," I said softly, lifting my eyes to meet his.

"*Mam* showed me how to crochet so I could make it myself. Do you really like it?"

My eyes filled with tears of joy. I swallowed hard around the lump that had found its way into my throat, then, kissed him with quivering lips.

"The fact that ya made it yourself makes it the most incredible gift I've ever gotten," I managed between tears and laughter.

We held each other tight; consequently, neither of us heard the squeak of the screen-door until it was too late. My father and Abraham were standing on the porch and had observed our lengthy embrace. Panic overtook me as I stepped away from Elijah. We both stood at attention while the two adult men remained silent for several minutes, staring us down.

Just when I thought I couldn't stand the silence any longer, Elijah's voice startled me.

"Mr. Reeves, I would like permission to court your daughter. I love Jane, and would never do anything to break her heart. I fully understand the meaning of commitment, and I intend to prove myself worthy of her hand."

"I believe ya, son," my father spoke authoritatively. "But ya need to understand that I set some rules down for my girls, and that includes no datin' or courtin' until they turn seventeen."

I began to shake and my palms nearly dripped with perspiration. Elijah reached a hand out to me and I instinctively took it.

"I understand that you have rules, sir. However, if I may be so bold, I would like ya to consider changing your mind for Jane and me."

Elijah spoke bravely, and with authority—like a man. He held my trembling hand even tighter, as though he were determined not to give up.

"We have discussed in great length the relationship that the two of you have developed," Abraham spoke. "It has been our determination through the close observance of our children, that you have shown that you are no longer children. You may have my blessing to court, if it pleases Jane's parents also."

I turned to my father with a pleading look on my face. "Daddy, please."

He smiled in defeat and nodded his consent. I felt so overwhelmed with love for both my father and Elijah that I didn't know which one to hug first. It was Elijah who decided for me, for he was holding me tight before I could gather my wits about me. The two men went back in the house, leaving Elijah and me alone. We stayed outside so long that our families ate dinner without us, but I didn't mind—my stomach was too full of butterflies, and my heart was full of love for Elijah.

As the great harvest moon peeked up over the horizon, I felt a chill in the air. This didn't concern me, for I had the warmth of a shawl made with love and the strong arms of the man I loved around me. Both of these would keep me, and my heart warm for a long time to come.

SIX
A TIME TO PREPARE

November arrived with bone-numbing sleet, creating icy patches along the hibernating soil. Gray clouds pushed their way across the frigid sky as though they were in a hurry, but the days seemed to stand still. It felt odd to be preparing for a wedding when winter storms were such a strong possibility this time of year. It was already so cold that Elijah hadn't taken me to the creek since our birthday. Instead, we would meet secretly in the loft of his barn. We were both still so unsure of our family's position on our relationship that we decided it best to keep a low profile. If my father knew just how much I loved Elijah he would probably keep too close an eye on us, and I enjoyed being alone with him—not because I intended to do anything wrong, but because of the way I felt when we were together. I'd liked a few boys at the public school back in my home town, but I'd never felt like this before. Being with Elijah felt natural, and I never had to force myself to think of things to say to him. He didn't intimidate me the way other boys had; he was a gentleman who genuinely cared to treat me with respect and true friendship.

I looked out at the rain as I grabbed my heavy raincoat and pulled on a pair of rubber boots from the mudroom. Nadine and I shared the boots, and usually only used them to fetch eggs from the chicken coop or to rake the hay in the barn. I didn't care how I looked in the boots; my only concern was the icy puddles that dominated the ground between where I stood and the Zook's barn.

Elijah was already waiting for me when I entered his barn.

"I was beginning to worry the rain would keep you from coming today."

"No way." I pulled off the raincoat and hung it on a nail near Eli's stall, then, climbed the ladder to the loft and kicked the boots against each other until they dropped in the haystack below. "I would never let a little rain keep me from seeing you."

Once I was settled in next to him, he kissed my cheek but I turned my head so I could kiss him fully on the mouth. With his mouth slightly open, I pressed my tongue lightly to his. He responded by doing the same. This was something different, and I liked it so much I continued to kiss him with a slightly open mouth, catching his tongue on mine every few kisses. Nadine had told me that she'd kissed a boy like this once, declaring how he'd practically slobbered all over her face. This was nothing like her horror story. It was almost like a dance that we were keeping perfect time with; a very rhythmic dance that was perfectly choreographed.

Before long, it grew dark in the barn, and it was time for us to leave each other. We hadn't even talked.

We'd spent the entire hour kissing—making out—as Nadine would call it. I didn't want to leave him, but I had to help my mother with the evening meal.

"I could kiss you forever."

Elijah smiled at me. "Don't worry, you will. We will be married and we will be able to kiss each other for the rest of our lives."

"That's cool. I like the sound of that."

"Go home, before I start kissing you again. I'm not sure I could stop if we started again."

I kissed him again on purpose just to test him.

He kissed back and held me so close it sent a rush of adrenaline through my entire body.

I knew then it was time to stop.

I jumped down from the loft and began to push my feet into my boots hoping to grab my coat and go before Elijah descended the ladder, but he grabbed me playfully and pulled me to him once more.

"I better not kiss you like that anymore if it's going to scare ya away like that."

"Ya didn't scare me away. I just can't afford to stay here and kiss ya for another hour. I get too caught up in ya, and my mamma will ground me if I don't get home. Then it will be a long time before I can kiss ya again, and I don't know if I can go even a day without kissin' ya."

He let me go so I could put my raincoat on.

"Then I won't kiss you again until tomorrow. I love you, Jane."

"I love you too, Elijah."

I walked out of the barn without turning back. I knew that if I looked in his blue eyes I'd want to kiss him, and I couldn't risk being grounded; not even for kisses as wonderful as we just shared.

ഇഇരു

The wedding grew near, and the weather colder. Rebekah worked diligently putting the finishing touches on her gown in time for the wedding. It was more like a dress than a gown, for Abraham had scolded her regarding the fancy dress her heart desired to make. He allowed her the long length and a frilly collar, but not the ruffled skirting to make the dress expand at the bottom. She was to have a plain, simple gown that reflected more the Old Order than the fancy ways of the world. She had argued with her father regarding a veil, but in the end; he gave in and allowed a simple veil. I feared that when my time came to marry Elijah, there would be an argument as to whether I would be allowed to wear a veil. I liked fancy things, and didn't think I liked the control the church could have over my wedding. I hoped that Nadine's stubbornness before me would change the unbending minds of the elder Amish men. Some of them had not yet fully accepted the freedom from the Old Order traditions, but instead, held fast to the strict rules of the Ordnung. My father explained that some of them were set in their ways, and hard pressed to change.

In the end, it was decided that a combination of traditions from both families would be incorporated into the wedding. It would be just fancy enough to satisfy Rebekah's desire to blend with Mitchell's upbringing, yet traditional enough to humor the majority of the Elders of the Ordnung. Meanwhile, Nadine and I scrambled to make our bridesmaid dresses for the upcoming day. My mother helped with the cutting, but the slowness of the pedal-operated Singer sewing machine certainly didn't help to speed up the process.

With so much to do before Mitchell's wedding, there was little time to spend with Elijah. When we did see each other, we kissed more than we talked, and I was falling more in love with him every day. We talked and planned of how we wanted our own wedding to be. He didn't protest when I voiced my desire to have a less simple gown than his sister's. He told me that he wanted me to have everything that would make me happy—including a veil. I felt fortunate to have such an understanding man for a future mate.

Nadine and I were to stand with Rebekah. Mitchell would have Elijah and Benjamin to stand with him. I was excited knowing that I would hold Elijah's arm as we walked down the aisle of the church, even if it wasn't the two of us who were getting married. What excited me even more was the barn dance that would follow the dinner. This would be my first opportunity to dance with Elijah, and I could scarcely wait.

The surrounding neighbors and family were a-buzz with planning the food for the wedding meal. The checklist was made, and Nadine and I were to assist Rebekah with all the final details. The women continued to sew the things for Rebekah's dowry, and clean the Zook's house in preparation for the wedding meal. The Bishop had "published" their upcoming Thursday wedding at the services on Sunday. With only two days left before the wedding, all that was left to do was to prepare the food.

Since the Zook's chose the Lapp family to do the serving of the wedding supper, they helped to prepare the food, but we all pitched in. The women made pies and peeled potatoes, while some of the men cleaned celery and cracked nuts. After a while, I helped Elijah with the nut cracking because I was sick of peeling potatoes. A few of the men were out making adjustments to the Zook's barn for the dance.

ↄ◌ʒ

At six o'clock in the morning the day of the wedding, Rebekah came over so that we could decide on a style in which to do our hair. Since we were each determined to wear our hair the same way, we tried for one style in particular. While the three of us crowded in the bathroom, my mother stood at the door in her usual spot, chuckling about our unreasonable quarrel. After noticing our increasing aggravation at each of us wanting our way, she held up a hand signaling us to be silent and pay some heed to her ever-so-sensible advice.

"Now, hold your horses young ladies. I think that we all will agree that your bickering is pointless. I think I'll take matters into my own hands," she advised, with a hint of laughter still present in her voice.

By this time, Naomi had entered the upstairs hall, making her presence known. After asking for a brief description of the hairstyle, she set to work with my mother so we could finish quicker. A *kapp* was placed on Nadine's head and then on mine, while the hair was maneuvered around it, leaving most of it showing—not traditional Amish style. Rebekah's hair looked the most beautiful with the ring of the veil surrounding the piles of reddish-brown curls that rested on top of her head. My mother and Naomi piled on the Dipity-Do to hold our hair in place. Having no mirrors in the Zook's house, Rebekah felt privileged to take advantage of seeing her hair take shape before her eyes in our mirror. She seemed to marvel at the sight of her beauty, and Naomi allowed the indulgence.

SEVEN
A TIME TO WED

At last, the time had come for the wedding to begin. We all arrived at the church at around the same time. I arranged and rearranged the pale green bow at the waistline of my cream colored dress as I waited for Elijah to join me in the entry hall of the church. Benjamin entered first, and I watched him swoon over Nadine as he kissed her softly on her lips. They were so lovable together I was convinced there was no one else on earth for either of them. It made me happy to see my older sister so much in love, but my heart leapt with excitement for my big brother, Mitchell. To finally be able to appreciate and love him was wonderful. To be proud of the way he turned his life from potential disaster made me whisper a small prayer of thanks.

Promptly at nine o'clock, Elijah entered the tiny hall with his sister on his arm. He looked proud as he walked with his older sister. Abraham then took his position at Rebekah's side with loving eyes that showed a hint of tears.

Elijah took his place at my side and kissed me gently on my cheek, while he gave my arm an excited squeeze. I felt happy and loved to be such a big part of the most important day in my brother's life.

Thoughts of my own wedding whirled around in my head, as I took Elijah's arm to follow behind Nadine and Benjamin down the aisle. I wondered how I would manage to convince Mr. Zook that it would be all right to have a fancier wedding than this one. The church was beautiful, but I wanted more flowers, and bows on the ends of the wooden pews. I envisioned my gown to be fancy with trailing lace. My bouquet would be overflowing with pink roses, instead of the daisies that made up Rebekah's primitive bouquet.

We took our places and turned to watch as Rebekah made her entrance from the back of the church. The look of pure joy on her face, made me realize that none of the fancy things mattered to her. Her rosy cheeks glowed as she kept her eyes on Mitchell the entire trip down the aisle of the church. I reached up a hand to touch the *kapp* that I was required to wear for the ceremony, and suddenly wondered why I had made such a fuss when Rebekah presented it to me.

A Bible verse came to mind as I tried to shake off my pride-full thoughts. *Your beauty should not come from outward adornment, such as braided hair and the wearing of gold jewelry and fine clothes. Instead, it should be that of your inner self, the unfading beauty of a gentle and quiet spirit, which is of great worth in God's sight. For this is the way the holy women of the past who put their hope in God used to make themselves beautiful.*

I reflected on the day that I had decided to memorize the verse from the scripture. It was from 1 Peter, and most memorably, the first day I had dared to quote scripture to my mother. I felt thankful for the strength God had given me to endure her harsh words nearly three years ago. Suddenly, I realized; had I given up that first day, I might not have known the happiness I now treasured in my constantly changing heart.

Elijah, Benjamin, Nadine and I took our places at the front pew, as Mitchell and Rebekah went to a private room to the side of the altar. The Bishop followed them through the door, where they would be given instructions relative to the marital duties of both parties. If they both consented, they would return to recite their vows. Hymns were sung in German from the *Ausbund* as we waited for their return.

At last, the couple made their appearance and the sermon began. The music stopped and I pushed aside my thoughts to pay attention to the wedding vows being exchanged between Mitchell and Rebekah.

The ceremony itself was incorporated in the sermon, and I found it rather difficult to follow. Mitchell, however, seemed to know exactly what to do and when to do it. I secretly hoped that Elijah would cue me when we got our chance at the altar.

The Bishop prompted the couple to answer if they were confident as to whether they were ordained by God to be husband and wife. Mitchell and Rebekah agreed in unison, broad smiles spreading across their faces. I quickly looked away from the Bishop in fear I might start giggling. I turned my attention to my mother and Naomi. They both had tears falling down their cheeks. I tried to get my mother's attention so that I could offer a consoling smile, but it seemed as if all that mattered to her was to make sure she wouldn't miss one single moment of Mitchell's wedding.

As the ceremony neared its end, the Bishop laid his hand over the clasped hands of the bride and groom and gave the blessing upon the newly wed couple. I turned my attention from my mother so I could hear the same words that would soon bind Elijah and me together.

"May the God of Abraham, Isaac and Jacob be with you to carry out the abounding blessing of married life, having made your vows before Him on this day. May the Lord's face shine upon the two of you. Go forth and be fruitful. In Jesus' name, Amen."

The kiss was simple and quick.

"May I present Mr. and Mrs. Mitchell Reeves," the Bishop finished. He then motioned for them to exit the church.

Everyone stood to sing the usual wedding hymn, while Elijah and I locked eyes, sending the silent message to one another that we were both eagerly anticipating our own wedding day.

Rebekah took Mitchell's arm and the two walked down the aisle followed by Benjamin and Nadine, then, Elijah and me. I locked onto Elijah's waiting arm as we exited the church to his waiting courting buggy. Mitchell and Rebekah were on their way, followed by Benjamin and Nadine in his courting buggy.

Elijah and I stayed behind for a few minutes to talk. Eli seemed impatient to pull the buggy, but Elijah held him in check.

"I have been waiting all day to tell ya how absolutely beautiful ya look," he said through a wide grin. He had turned to face me, and now looked deep into my eyes. Grabbing the sides of my face, he pulled me to him and kissed me several times. Then he reached back and unpinned the kapp from my head, and threw it in the back of the buggy.

"There, now that's much better, *jah?* Now I can see more of your beautiful hair."

His remarks caused me to blush, and I cast my eyes downward. He lifted my chin to make me look at him.

"Don't be embarrassed by the things I say to you. I love you, and I think you're beautiful."

"I'm sorry," I said humbly. "I suppose I haven't ever been able to take compliments very well. My mother used to call me a lot of bad names, and it made me feel ugly and unwanted, I guess."

"Don't apologize. But I know your *mam* is good to ya now, so there isn't any reason for ya to be insecure anymore. Give your hurts to God. He loves ya more than I do—and that's a *gut* amount."

"I know that, but over the years, the bad stuff has just been easier to believe," I said solemnly.

He held me close for a time, stroking my hair and kissing my temples.

Then, grabbing the reigns, he clucked at Eli prompting him to trot. Our course was set for the Zook farm, where the wedding supper awaited our arrival.

Mitchell and Rebekah reached the farm way ahead of us, and they went to her bedroom upstairs. Their wedding gifts had been placed on her bed, where the couple admired them. When Elijah and I arrived, we headed up the stairs to alert the newlyweds that the meal was due to be served soon. Our timing was right on cue, for we walked in the room just in time to catch them kissing romantically. Our intrusion appeared to embarrass Rebekah because she covered her blushing face and giggled when she noticed us.

"We'll be down in a minute, Jane. Thanks for lettin' us know," Mitchell said.

Dinner lasted nearly two hours by the time all the guests had been served. I began to get impatient for the barn dance to commence. Elijah seemed to pick up on my mood, and excused the two of us from the company of my brother and his bride.

Outside, the air was a little crisp, but not enough to see a full breath of air when you breathed out through your mouth. Elijah led me to the barn, which had been closed off for days in preparation for the festivities that would soon take place. Inside, lanterns hung above our heads for light, and the barn doors served to protect against the wind. It was quite warm in the shelter of the large barn, and I knew it would only get warmer with the number of bodies that would soon fill it.

Tables were set up in the loft for guests to have refreshments of punch and the wedding cake that lay before us on a separate table. Mitchell had requested a separate wedding cake to be eaten aside from the usual pies and pastries that were being served in the house with the dinner itself. At the far end of the barn, a makeshift stage had been assembled which would serve for the playing of musical instruments.

Elijah stepped onto the platform, and picked up a stringed instrument. He began to strum it beautifully, much to my surprise. I was amazed at his talented efforts with the instrument. After he played an unrecognizable tune, he bowed slightly, causing me to giggle.

"That was wonderful!" I said, clapping at his performance. "I had no idea ya had that kinda talent."

"My papa instructed me from the time I was a tiny tot. He felt it important to pass on his abilities to Samuel and me. This is his banjo, but I hope to get my own someday."

"I thought Amish didn't play instruments."

"Normally they don't, but I suppose we've been more Mennonite than Amish. My grandfather was Mennonite, so my papa and his siblings never had the strict upbringing that some in the community have had. But since our Bishop also denounced the Old Order a few years back, the community has allowed music and barn dances— especially in the spring after everyone has been cooped up most of the winter."

"My mamma can play our piano with such grace; you'd have thought she was born playin'. She has tried to teach me to play and read music, but I don't seem to have the ear for it—much less the patience. At Christmas, when she plays Silent Night, it's almost haunting the way she plays because it sounds the same as when my grandmother used to play it."

Elijah looked at me lovingly, and began to play a slower tune. One by one, the wedding guests filed into the barn, filling it with talk and laughter. Elijah handed the banjo to his brother, while the other players picked up the harmonica, guitar and violin. Elijah stepped off the platform and reached for my hand as the instruments brought forth a soft tune.

"May I have the first dance?" he asked politely.

I nodded a shy response, and we began a slow, clumsy, would-be waltz.

I had never danced this way before, but the movements seemed to come easily after a few minutes.

"You dance beautifully," Elijah whispered in my ear.

"That's a good thing ya think that, b'cause I've never done this b'fore," I admitted.

He didn't seem to care. He smiled, and continued to hold me as we floated around the barn floor like dandelion seedlings. After a few tries at the square dancing, I gave up, allowing Elijah to take a turn on stage with the banjo. Samuel sat with me, as I admired my future husband and his talent with the instrument.

The night wore on, filled with talking and dancing. Soon, Elijah was beside me once more as his father took a turn with the banjo. They each played wonderfully, but I was partial to Elijah's playing because of my deep love for him. A thought occurred to me as I watched the merriment of the over-crowded barn.

"My father told me b'fore we moved here that Amish people don't dance either."

"Our *Ordnung* has always been quite liberal with barn dances and the wearing of colors. I suppose our liberal attitude contributed to our recent change over to true salvation."

"Didn't ya have Jesus b'fore ya got saved?"

"*Jah*, we always had a grasp on who Jesus was, but we concentrated more on the rules of the *Ordnung* and our humble way of life and works, than on the gift of salvation."

"Ya mean ya didn't obey God either?"

"No, that's not what I meant. We observed more the rules of the *Ordnung*, rather than studying the Bible and living strictly by the Word of God," he explained. "So it was a way of life according to the rules of the *Ordnung*?"

"*Jah*. God has set us free from being under the law of the *Ordnung*. Our works alone would not have saved us, and we know that now," he said cheerfully.

"Let's dance again b'fore the music stops playin' for the night," I suggested, changing the subject.

We entered the designated dance area, and I spotted something that held my attention for a minute.

"What is so interesting across the room that has ya so distracted?"

His voice almost seemed to carry a hint of playful jealousy regarding what was taking my attention away from him.

"Is it just me, or does it seem that lately Hannah and David Yoder have been gettin' a little chummy? Have ya noticed it, too?" I asked.

Elijah looked down at me with a smile that was playing largely on his lips.

"Truth is, I've thought the same thing, and even inquired of David about the subject. Each time, he denies it in an embarrassed and defensive manner. But, never once have I met an Amish boy willing to admit he is courting someone."

He continued speaking playfully.

"But you know I will always be glad to admit to the fact that you are my girl—my little wild flower—because I love ya for sure and for certain!"

He was still grinning as we stepped away from the designated dance floor when the music stopped playing. I was glad to hear that he would never deny loving me.

It soon became time for the festivities to come to an end. I felt sad that my time with Elijah would be over, but I was extremely tired from the full day that we had.

As the party wound down to an end, Elijah wrapped the shawl that he made around my shoulders. The time was nearing midnight, but we loitered under the big oak tree between our properties. We held hands and kissed, as we discussed our future plans for our own marriage.

"How soon will your papa allow us to marry?" Elijah asked

"I hope it'll be soon. I'm not sure how long I can wait. Ya know, it's kinda funny, but I never thought I'd be wantin' to get married at sixteen."

It was a new concept to me, true, but it felt like an acceptable one—something I could certainly get used to.

"I'd like it if ya married me just after I turn eighteen. That's less than a year—not too long to wait."

His words were comforting, but the real task would be in convincing my parents I was mature enough to marry at seventeen.

"If they allow Nadine to marry Benjamin b'fore she turns eighteen; that will work in my favor."

The look on his face gave me the impression that he wasn't as optimistic as I was.

"I have a few things to take care of before we can get married," he explained.

"Like what?"

"I'd like to wait a little longer before I tell ya, if ya wouldn't mind. It's a surprise that Papa and I started working on a couple of weeks ago."

The mischievous smile on his face made me wonder just what he was up to, but I wouldn't dream of spoiling it for him.

"I love you so much."

Elijah drew me closer, sheltering me from the wind that threatened to force us back into the barn.

"I'm hoping that it will be our turn, come next November. If we could start planning for that time, I'd be the happiest man in the world!"

His excitement encouraged me to eagerly pursue the permission I needed from my parents. However, I would first wait on the outcome of Nadine's request for marrying Benjamin. If she could persuade our parents to give in to her marrying Benjamin while she was still seventeen, it could change their minds for me, too. After all, I would turn seventeen the same day Elijah turned eighteen. One month later, in November, we could marry if we could get the permission that we sought. There would be a lot to get done in the short year before our wedding could take place, though.

ଥଔଓଷ

Mitchell and Rebekah visited relatives for a few weeks before settling into the *Dawdi Haus* out back of our property. My father gave Mitchell two acres of land that adjoined a plot that consisted of a ten-acre field that was for sale. Mitchell was already in the process of making it his through a bank loan. The acres that my father gave to him were for building his own house for his new wife and future children. The men in the community had already begun to help him get the main structure up before winter set in. The outside structure would be constructed in the same fashion as a barn-raising, but the detail work inside would be Mitchell's sole responsibility.

ଥଔଓଷ

By the end of February, Rebekah discovered she was pregnant with the first grandchild for both sides of the family. Everyone was thrilled. Deborah Yoder seemed to be more excited than any of our family because she had been taking over the school teaching in Rebekah's absence, and she wanted the job full time. Rebekah suffered from so much morning sickness, it had lasted nearly all day for several weeks. My mother suggested she must be having a girl, since in her opinion girls seem to cause more hormonal disturbances. Naomi claimed to be sick with each of her pregnancies, so she couldn't offer any argument for or against my mother's statement.

My father allowed Nadine to officially quit school even though she hadn't really participated as a student for a few months. She assisted Deborah in her efforts to take over the teaching of Rebekah's students, allowing her to make the decision as to whether she should resign from her position. In Nadine's absence, I decided I would beg my mother to let me quit, too. She knew I hadn't learned anything new since I'd attended because it had been nothing but review of my past years at the public school. Since the Amish didn't plan for their students to be instructed past the eighth grade, it was difficult to learn anything new in their school.

When I presented the facts to my mother, she understood that I wanted to be the wife of an Amish farmer, thus making it a moot point to continue boring myself with review. With her increasing responsibilities due to the recent birth of my brother, Samuel, she welcomed the help I could give at home. My duties mainly consisted of taking the responsibility for three-year-old Molly. On washday, I washed all of baby Sammy's diapers and Nadine helped with the family laundry after her teaching duties.

After much debate, Rebekah turned over the classroom to Deborah full time. She did not feel that her difficult pregnancy would allow her to finish the school year. Deborah was getting the hang of things, which allowed Nadine more time at home to help me with Molly and the chores.

Having lunch with Elijah most days was a good break from the stress that I had so willingly accepted. I didn't regret my decision to quit school to help my mother; it simply was a lot of adjusting to make at one time.

EIGHT
A TIME TO WAIT

With the arrival of spring, came a yearning in Nadine that nothing but marrying Benjamin could satisfy. She was as determined as ever to shake things up in the Amish community by demanding that she be able to marry in June, right in the middle of planting season. She insisted that by May the planting should be done, so by June, there shouldn't be much else to do except sit back and watch the corn grow. I found the whole thing comical the way she presented it, but a few of the elders didn't seem to take too kindly to the whole idea.

ಐ⊙ಐ

Before any of us knew what happened, we were planning Nadine's June wedding—to be held outside. This was definitely a first in the history of the community, but the whole thing was too exciting not to take part in.

Besides, Nadine was too much of a flower child to have anything but a June wedding. I was envious of my sister in addition to my happiness for her. I wanted the time to speed up to my own wedding. I felt so impatient at times, I worried I wouldn't be able to contain myself.

The preparations for Nadine's and Benjamin's wedding were nearly ready, and the time came for the "publishing" by the Bishop at the Sunday services. Some of the people who weren't aware of the upcoming event seemed a little put off by it, but accepted it, nonetheless. To make things easier, I would wear the same dress that I wore for Rebekah's wedding. It was lovely, and I'd only used it for church a few times after her wedding. Elijah was always happy to see me in the dress, so it made me happy to wear it any occasion I could.

"It's our turn next," Elijah whispered to me while we waited for Nadine to make her entrance at the back of the waiting crowd that had turned out to witness the biggest event of the community's history.

An aisle had been formed from rows of rented, fold-up chairs that were set up in the flower garden behind the Lapp's house. Nadine had insisted that this was the perfect spot for the outdoor wedding. I had to agree as I looked around at the vined trellis and the sun that shined flawlessly in the cloudless sky.

"I don't know if I can wait that long," I whispered back to Elijah.

Elijah and I smiled at each other until the time came for us to start walking down the aisle. David Yoder and Hannah Lapp also served as attendants, but we were first to walk to the front of the makeshift altar, where the couple would be joined. The wedding seemed to drag on, giving me plenty of time to let my mind wander.

At last, they were married and we followed them out of the crowd of chairs that lined the aisle. Before we rode off, Hannah stopped me to speak privately.

"I wanted you to be the first to know that David Yoder and I have decided to get married at the end of August, right after I turn seventeen, but just before harvest!"

Her face was flush, and she could scarcely contain her giddy smile. At first, I didn't know how to react. I felt happiness for my friend; and jealousy at the same time. Not wanting to be overtaken with the jealousy, I offered her a sincere congratulations, and gave her a squeeze.

"I am so happy for ya," I squealed. "Oh, but I do wish that it could be me that was getting married! Oh, but I'm so happy for ya."

I meant it—every word of it. She was my best friend, and nothing could make me get in the way of her happiness. We hugged and cried, as we giggled in-between wiping our tears. Benjamin had told Elijah about the upcoming wedding at the same time the two of us were blubbering about it the way girls do. They walked over to us, and Elijah grabbed my hand and held it tight. I knew he was thinking the same thing I was—when was it ever going to be our turn?

That evening at the wedding dinner, Elijah boldly went to my father and officially asked for my hand in marriage. Although he consented, he insisted that we wait until after I would turn seventeen.

"I appreciate your boldness, Elijah," my father said. "I give ya my consent, but ya have to wait until she turns seventeen."

My father was turning into such a pushover.

"Thank you, Sir," was all Elijah said before grabbing my hand and whisking me away from the crowd.

I walked fast behind Elijah, who was practically pulling me along. Once we reached the rows of chairs that the guests had used to observe the wedding, he motioned me to sit on the outside of the aisle. Breathlessly, he knelt on one knee before me and took my right hand in his.

"I love you so much, Jane," he said around the tears that fell unchecked from his blue eyes.

I didn't say a word, but began to weep quietly, for I knew what was about to happen. We both stared into each other's eyes, weeping quietly for a moment.

"I never thought this day would come," he finally managed to say. "You are the most precious thing to me aside from my Savior. I want you to be second to Him in my life."

He wiped a tear that clung to my cheek and smiled a heart-felt smile.

"I would like to spend the rest of my life loving you as your husband. Will you honor me by marrying me and being my wife for the remainder of our days?"

"Yes, Elijah," I whispered.

Elijah let out a whoop, pulling me into his arms to claim me as his own. For the first time, I really felt that I would finally get my chance to be Mrs. Elijah Zook, and I felt nothing would ever make me happier than that.

ಬಃಂ

Time moved quickly, and before we knew it, Hannah's wedding was only two days away. She asked Deborah and me to stand up with her, and we both graciously accepted. Since we knew Deborah wasn't courting anyone, Hannah and I had put our heads together for days trying to find someone suitable to escort her. It was David who finally suggested Matthew Beiler, though he was a bit older than she. David and I decided that it would be best that his twin sister not suspect that we were setting her up with Matthew. Hannah and I decided they were perfectly suited for one another, but they just hadn't become aware of it yet.

⊱⊰

At the wedding, neither Matthew, nor Deborah protested when Elijah and I arranged them in line together. Even though Hannah was too busy at her wedding to notice the mutual admiration between Deborah and Matthew, Elijah and I hadn't missed it one bit. David also took the time to notice, and I commended him on a job well done in helping me set the whole thing up.

⊱⊰

As the excitement wound down at the end of the wedding supper, I began to have a few mixed feelings. I watched Hannah with her new husband, and began to realize that my friendship with her would be taking second seat to her new life as a wife. Things were changing so quickly. We were all growing up, and I was being thrust into the adult world with full force. Mitchell and Nadine were married, and I was about to become an aunt and even a wife soon. My heart fluttered a little as I stepped away from Elijah. I began to walk out of the Lapp home, feeling the need for some fresh air. Elijah was right on my heels.

"What's wrong with my little wild flower?" he asked.

I suddenly came to a halt and Elijah stopped short of running in to me.

"I guess things just started to overwhelm me a little. Everything is movin' so fast. I'm growin' up so fast—and my brother and sister are both married people now. Mitchell is gonna be a papa pretty soon. I wonder if he's scared, ya know?"

All my thoughts were coming out at once and I had to admit, I felt quite overwhelmed. Elijah held me tight and didn't speak a word. He smoothed my hair and comforted me as I wept to release my feelings of stress. When I calmed down some, he lifted my chin to show me the smile on his face that seemed to be waiting for me all along.

"I love you so much."

"I love you too, Elijah."

"Do you remember that surprise I was telling ya about?" he asked, his face beaming. "I was planning on waiting until it was finished so I could show ya on our birthday, but I think you need to see it now. I'm not sure I can wait another five weeks to show you. We can go quickly and be back before anyone even misses us."

I nodded and he led me to his courting buggy and unhitched Eli from it, offering me a boost on the horse. His strong arms cradled me as he mounted the horse behind me. With a click from Elijah, the horse set off trotting in the direction his owner steered him.

"So where are we goin'? Is it far?"

"You'll see, and it will be worth every bit of your anticipation," he said.

We traveled the remainder of the journey without speaking as Elijah guided the horse down the lane that led to the far fields of the Zook's property. As we reached the top of a hill, I surveyed the valley down below, until my eyes focused on a newly built house at the bottom of the hill. Elijah kept the horse trotting in the course that led to the house, and I was too afraid to think what I wanted to think. We stopped in front of the house, and Elijah jumped off the horse to assist me.

"Okay, ya got me. Who lives here?"

I was almost afraid of the answer that Elijah was seemingly hesitant to offer.

"This, my love, is the house that I have been building for us to live in after we are married."

"Uh, uh. You can't be serious. This is totally righteous."

"Is that a good thing?'

"This must have cost you a lot of bread. Are ya sure this is for us?"

He smiled his answer, and I jumped into his arms, showering him with kisses. I held him for several minutes, while the reality sunk in.

"Well, come on. Don't ya want to see the inside?" he asked with excitement in his voice.

"Of course I do," I laughed, wiping the tears from my eyes. "But where did ya get the money to pay for all this?"

"I have been saving my money from the roadside stand where I sell my vegetables since I was nine years old."

"Why did ya spend it all on me?"

"Because I love you my little wild flower. I saved the money for my future, and you are my future."

Suddenly without warning, Elijah scooped me up in his arms and carried me up on the porch of the house.

"Let me down. Shouldn't ya wait 'till we're married first?"

"I can't wait any longer. I've waited too long already, and ya have to be carried in the house the first time ya see it. Do ya have any idea how tough it's been keeping this from ya?"

There seemed to be a slight amount of tension in his voice—enough to let me know how painful his unintended deception was. He continued to hold me, in spite of my constant protest. Into the house we went before he let me stand on my own two feet.

I surveyed the front room with hands held to my mouth in awe of its welcoming allure.

The beauty of the woodwork nearly took my breath away. It was apparent that this was truly a labor of love. It was a work of art, and my Elijah was its creator.

"Oh my! You've given me the most precious thing anyone has ever given me, 'cept for God and Mamma and Daddy givin' me my very life."

I ran my hand along the solid oak banister of the stairway, admiring the smoothness of the glossy finish on the wood. I felt compelled to tour the upstairs first, so I walked up to the first landing and paused to invite Elijah to join me in exploring our new house together. Each room offered extraordinary little alcoves, and closets—much to my surprise. After skipping two rooms across from each other that were closed off, he led me into the master bedroom. Much to my delight and amazement, it had a full working bathroom with a claw-foot tub and a separate shower.

"Oh Elijah, how did ya get yer papa to agree to let us have a real bathroom?" I asked excitedly.

"We can talk about that later. Wait until ya see the rest of the house. There are a lot more surprises in store for ya downstairs."

The rooms with the closed doors turned out to be additional bathrooms. Altogether, the upstairs had five bedrooms and three bathrooms. The front room contained homemade rocking chairs and tables with oil lamps seated neatly atop. When I asked Elijah, he confirmed that he and his father had made the beautiful pieces. The kitchen was filled with various sizes of missionary style cabinets, and before a large bay window, stood a table and eight chairs that matched the wood and style of the cupboards.

"Don't tell me ya made the cabinets and the table, too?" I questioned him.

"*Jah*. Homemade is so much nicer, don't ya think?"

"How did ya ever have the time to do all this?"

"I did most of it while you were preoccupied with Nadine's and Hannah's wedding preparations. The rest, I did a little here and a little there. I've been working on it ever since your papa gave us permission to court. From that time on, marrying you was my focus for getting this done," he confessed. "Besides, you know the men in the community helped—the house itself went up fast."

I stood for a moment, staring at the reflection of the furniture in the shine of the hardwood floors.

"I can't believe ya put in wood floors. This is so beautiful."

"All I did was picture the things you told me about that ya loved so much about the house ya grew up in, and I tried to add those things in the home you will be spending the rest of your life in," he said as he leaned in behind me and rested his chin on my shoulder.

A smile crossed his face as he watched me admire his handiwork. I couldn't help but praise him repeatedly for his talent in building our home. It almost made me feel glad

that he had kept it from me because I may have gotten in
his way and delayed him.

"Oh, this is so beautiful; I don't ever want to leave!
I wish we could move in right now."

He shared my enthusiasm, and openly expressed his
eagerness to be wed to me.

"How will I ever be able to go back to my small
little space in my parent's house, when I have this waitin'
for me?"

"You can come here any time ya like. This is our
home. While I'm finishing up the walls, maybe I could
persuade you to make some curtains," he smiled as he
nudged me playfully. "Making curtains was the one thing
papa and I couldn't do. *Mam* offered, but I figured that was
something you would want to do personally."

"Thanks for thinkin' of me."

I didn't have anything else I could say. There was
so much that I wanted to say, but I couldn't. I simply didn't
have the words to express my feelings for what he had done
for us—for our future.

"Ya don't have to thank me. This is just as much
your home as it is mine."

"Can I ask one thing?"

I was hesitant to ask, mostly because I feared his
answer.

"What is it that ya want to know?"

"Well," I hesitated further. "I was wondering what
all the bedrooms are for."

"The bedrooms are for filling with the children we
will have," he said with a robust grin.

I hadn't thought about children. I'd thought a lot
about how they were made, but not so much about being
pregnant, or bein' a mamma.

"How many do ya plan on havin' anyway?"

"At least six," he said, laughing.

What did I get myself into?

"You're kiddin', right?"

I felt a sudden difficulty in breathing.

"I think we should have as many as God intends to bless us with," he said, putting on his humble grin. "All I did was build the amount of bedrooms I felt led to by the Lord."

This answer I was willing to accept, although the thought of being responsible for six children left me feeling a little worried.

Shadows moved across the solid oak floors as the sun moved to the western horizon. It was getting late, and we'd missed a considerable amount of the wedding party. David and Hannah would surely have missed us by this late hour.

"We should get back," I offered. I didn't want to leave, but we were missing out on an important day for our friends.

"You're right. We haven't exactly been courteous to our friends," he agreed. "Just one more room to see, then we can go."

He flashed me a mischievous look as he took me by the hand.

Behind a set of French doors was the room he led me to. It was, in my opinion, the prettiest room in the house. I could understand why he'd saved it for the last one to be viewed. At the far end of the room stood a handsome fireplace, surrounded by bookcases on each side, reaching to the corners of the wall on both sides. The mantle was made of oak, as were the bookshelves. The main wall consisted of tall windows and two sets of French doors that led out to a brick patio. I twirled the skirting of my dress as I whirled around the large, open room.

"This is the most beautiful house I've ever seen! Thanks for building it for us."

"I can't wait until you're Mrs. Zook, and this house is filled with the laughter of children," he said.

I blushed slightly, but Elijah was too busy pulling me close to him to notice. He held me firmly and kissed me passionately. I kissed him back for several minutes with such fervor that he pulled me gently from him.

"If we're not careful, we're going to get ourselves into some trouble," he said. "We need to be more rational—more mature than this. I enjoy holding ya and kissing ya so much that, sometimes, I don't want to stop. Right now, though, I think we should stop because I'm feeling some strong urges to keep on holding you. I don't want us to do anything that we should be waiting for until after we're married. There's plenty of time for that after we're husband and wife."

He was right, I knew. I was having some intense feelings of my own. In recent years, I'd learned through reading the scriptures, the importance of remaining a virgin until marriage. I had remained pure this long, and didn't want to throw it all away in a moment of passion— especially with the man I intended to marry. I would be his for the rest of our lives and a few more months were not too long to wait.

Lord God, please help us to resist this temptation, I prayed silently. *Give us strength to wait....* Before I could finish, Elijah held both of my hands in his and began to pray aloud.

"Heavenly Father, we thank you for the opportunity to love one another. We are grateful for your love for us.

Help us to return that love to you by abstaining from a physical relationship until you bless our union with the covenant of marriage. Bless us with the strength to endure the time before our wedding, and keep our relationship strong and pure in you. In the mighty name of Jesus, Amen."

"Amen," I whispered through the lump that had formed in my throat.

His prayer had moved me to a higher level of love and respect for him. Knowing that Elijah loved me enough to keep our love pure until marriage made me love him all the more. Our purity was truly as important to him as it was to me—it was a sure sign that I would never doubt his love for me. It also gave me the desire to want to do things God's way—not by my own selfish, fleshly ways.

"I love you so much more because of the tough test we just endured. I think we let the situation with the house go to our heads a little. We just got through our first crisis as a couple, and came out the victor," he continued. "Let's lift our chins and return to the party. After defeating temptation, I'm ready for some wholesome fun. That was mighty draining, but we did it."

His voice reflected cheer and hope, which in turn, caused me to feel the same.

We clutched one an others' arms and left the house. The ride back to the Lapp's house was quiet. There wasn't anything else to be said, and I was content just to be in his company. When we arrived, everyone was too busy either playing a game, or talking in groups to notice us walking in the door—or so I thought. Nadine grabbed me almost immediately and pulled me away from Elijah to talk to me.

"Where have the two of you been all this time?" she asked harshly.

"Oh, Nadine," I said excitedly, "you're not gonna b'lieve what just happened. Elijah said he had a s'prise for me, and guess what it was?"

"Oh, I dunno—a house," she said, annoyance reflecting in her tone.

I scrunched my face into a frown. "How'd ya know?"

"Benjamin helped him with some haulin' of the wood and wall board from the hardware store in town. Dad and Mitchell helped with the roof."

"Ya mean ya knew all this time and ya didn't rat him out?"

"Nope. It was too important to Elijah that he get most of it done b'fore he showed it to ya. I thought he was gonna wait 'till both of yer birthdays to show it to ya. How come he didn't wait?"

"I was feelin' a little down about bein' the only one not married b'sides Deborah. I guess the whole wedding situation made me feel a little overwhelmed. So, he thought it would cheer me up some. It isn't finished yet, but it sure is beautiful. Have ya seen it?"

"Yes, I saw it. You're a lucky woman."

"Did you just call me a woman?"

"Yeah, I did, but don't let it go to yer head," Nadine said stubbornly.

I couldn't help but smile. "I'm a woman."

Nadine flashed me her most annoyed look. "Dream on."

"Don't be such a downer, Nadine."

"And maybe you should stop being such a fake, Jane."

I put my hands on my hips, ready to fight with my sister. "What do ya mean by that?"

She put her hands on her hips and stepped into my personal space, but I held my ground.

"What do ya think it means, Jane? It means you're a big fat fake when yer around Elijah."

"No more than you are when you're around Benjamin."

"Only 'cause I'm trying to hide our past from him."

"I guess I do it to spare Elijah about our past too. But that just shows how grown up I am."

"Yer right, Jane. I'm sorry. Yer definitely growing up to be a woman."

I felt so happy that she'd recognized the fact that I'd grown up, that I gave her a big hug. The rest of it didn't matter

"How're things in the Lapp home?" I asked when we let go of one another.

"Now that Hannah will be leavin' to live in the Yoder house, it's gonna be quiet with just Lydia left. Hannah and her younger sister used to get into a spat or two, now and then. The house will remain quiet for a little while because Benjamin and I decided that we would wait to try to have kids of our own for another couple a months—'till after I turn eighteen."

"Do ya mind livin' in his parent's house?" I asked cautiously.

"It's a nice home, and his folks are happy to live in the *Dawdi Haus*. B'sides, they're hopin' we can fill all the bedrooms with lots of children. Feel sorry for Hannah—she has to live with Deborah, unless we can get her married off to Matthew Beiler!"

We both laughed. It wasn't kind, but we both knew that unless Deborah had a distraction, Hannah would have a tough time living with her new sister-in-law until they could get their own house built. I looked across the room to spy on the new couple. They both seemed happy and talkative. Deborah caught me watching her and Matthew, and walked over to where Nadine and I were standing.

"*Denki*", she said with a squeal. "Matthew said he likes me, and it's a right *gut* thing because I like him, too. I'm so glad that you and my brother pushed us together. I think he's going to ask to court me—he keeps hinting," she said excitedly.

She was practically jumping up and down by this time, and I found myself joining in her excitement. I waved to Hannah across the room to come join us. When she walked over to us, I didn't even let Deborah talk. Instead, I spoke on her behalf.

"Matthew is gonna ask to court Deborah," I said, continuing to giggle.

"I *think* he's going to," Deborah corrected me.

The four of us hugged and squealed a little. Elijah, Benjamin, David and Matthew, who were all standing together, looked over at us. I knew by the looks on their faces they were probably wondering what had caused us to be so giddy. We didn't care what anyone thought—we just continued to laugh, enjoying our time with each other.

NINE
A TIME TO NEST

Time spent at my soon-to-be residence helped to fill the time that I would have to wait before my wedding. My mother took me shopping in town to buy the material I needed to make curtains for the house. We also purchased some beautiful material to make my wedding dress. Deborah Yoder and Miriam Miller would stand up with me. Alongside of them would be Matthew Beiler and Jonathan Zook, Elijah's cousin.

My mother was busy once again with Naomi, holding a quilting bee for me. We used some of the leftover swatches from my birthday dress and my bridesmaid dress to give the quilt more of a sentimental value. There was only one small piece of the material from the first dress that she made for me, so we put it in the very center of the quilt.

It seemed almost unreal to me that I would be married soon. Elijah was busy working the land that his father had given him. His furniture-making business that he was trying to establish, and his normal daily chores, kept us from having too much time alone in our house. He spent a lot of time in the barn that was still unfinished, while I put the finishing touches on the inside of the house. Nadine and my friends helped me with the curtains and the braided rugs that would serve for warmth against the coldness of the wooden floors in winter. The house was nearly furnished, except for the dishes, and linens we counted on getting as wedding gifts. We had a few dishes in the house— mismatched pieces from a few of my mother's and Naomi's old sets, but we would need a full service if we were ever to be able to entertain family and friends.

Elijah was expecting a few heads of cattle from his papa, while my mother offered to give me most of her chickens. She never did seem to get used to them—said she didn't want them for anything other than egging, but I'd grown quite fond of them over the past few years. My father and Mitchell did the butchering, while Nadine and I blanched and plucked them. My mother didn't have the stomach for it, and it wasn't one of my favorite chores either, even though I'd been doing it for as long as we had lived on the farm. Elijah assured me that he would take care of all the butchering of the livestock once we got married and that was cool with me.

ဆၢၔ

By the end of September, Nadine and I had finished the canning of all the fruit, jams and vegetables with my mother and Naomi. Between the two family gardens and what Nadine had from her first garden, we had enough to split between the four households. I was grateful, yet surprised, when they gave me an even share of the canned foods. My mother said it was for the help I gave; said she couldn't have done her fair share if it hadn't been for me taking a turn at diverting baby Sammy's attention away from the heat of the kitchen.

At the end of our final canning day, I took my filled Mason jars over to my own house to store them in the pantry. With food in the pantry, the house was nearly ready for its occupants. In another few weeks, the livestock and chickens would bring the noises of a busy farm to our place. The barn already housed Eli, and my mums were blooming just outside the front porch, making it look like home.

⛨⛨

October brought many changes and new beginnings for all of us. Rebekah was due to have her baby any time, and Mitchell was frantic. The two "visited" quite often. In fact, they were at our house and the Zook's more often than they were home. Rebekah and my mother would often sit by the fire in the cold evenings and sip cocoa while having long talks. Rebekah spent a lot of time admiring Sammy, and watching my mother closely while she cared for him. Rebekah's twin sisters, Mary and Elizabeth, were already a year old; not needing the same constant care and gentleness that baby Sammy still required.

"I haven't said anything to Mitchell, but I'm a little scared to take care of an infant on my own," Rebekah admitted to my mother nervously. "Oh, I've been there for *Mam* and everything, but I've never had to be the sole caregiver before. When we delivered the twins, I was shaking in my shoes," she admitted further.

"You'll do fine. We all do. We're all first time mothers at one time in our lives. You'll make mistakes and you'll learn from them—that is that," my mother assured her.

"Well one thing's for sure, I'm *gut* at washing diapers," she laughed.

"You're going to be a natural, you'll see," my mother encouraged her.

"I want a girl. I mean, I'll be happy with whatever God decides to bless me with, but I'm hoping for a girl."

The smile didn't leave Rebekah's face as she ran her hand gently along her swelled abdomen. When she spoke of her baby, her expression confirmed her love for the child and anticipation of the impending birth.

While my mother busied herself putting Sammy to sleep, I offered to get Rebekah a glass of milk. No sooner had I started pouring the milk, than Rebekah's call from the other room startled me.

"Jane, come here, quickly! Feel her, she's kicking!"

I walked swiftly to where she was sitting and placed my hand where she directed me. We both laughed while the baby poked and hiccupped. Elijah entered the room, and we straightened up momentarily, then, burst out laughing again.

"What is so funny?" he asked, looking down at his clothing to check for possible reasons for our laughter.

"It ain't you, silly," I said, laughing at him. "Your sister's baby has the hiccups."

"I don't see how that could be funny. The poor little guy probably has a stomach ache by now, and you two are laughing," he said sternly.

"Elijah, your *niece* has stopped hiccupping and seems to be settled down now, so stop worrying about *her,*" Rebekah said in the same tone Elijah used.

"I'm just kidding with ya, Rebekah. I didn't mean to ruffle your feathers."

He walked over and gave his sister an apologetic kiss on her forehead, then turned to me.

"Jane, could we take a ride over to the new house? I've got the buggy waiting out front."

Elijah seemed almost impatient, so I kissed my sister-in-law and gave her a strong hug so I could leave with her brother.

"Rebekah, I enjoyed the talk," I said.

I turned before walking out the door, and gave her a small wave of my hand.

Elijah took the long, scenic lane toward our soon-to-be home, allowing Eli to travel at a slow trot. The wind blew gently, playing with the curls along the sides of my cheeks. I pushed back my hair to admire the array of colors that clothed the trees along the path. The sun had descended just enough to add a chill to the air, causing me to pull my shawl tightly around me.

We reached the house before the wind picked up its pace, adding more crispness to the evening sunset. The colors that streamed across the sky now resembled the leaves that decorated the trees.

Elijah put Eli in the barn to protect him against the gusts of wind that threatened to bring rain. I went inside to start a fire in the fireplace so we could stay warm. By the time the fire was crackling, I had made us cocoa when Elijah came in from the barn.

"It's starting to drizzle, "Elijah said as he snuggled up behind me.

He placed his chilled hands on my neck, causing me to jump and spill a little of the cocoa on the floor. "I'm sorry, I'll clean it up," he said.

"You're right ya will," I said with a smirk.

He took the dishtowel and wiped the small spill before I could protest his choice of cleaning tool. I decided not to voice my slight unhappiness with him for using a clean dishtowel on the floor. It could be washed, so it wasn't such a big problem as to bicker over it. My mother had told me that it was best if I learned to pick my battles when dealing with a husband or children. I made up my mind to do just that because I knew I could sometimes be a bit more particular about things than most everyone else seemed to be.

I put the dirty dish towel away while Elijah pulled the quilts from the cedar chest in the hall. He placed them in front of the fireplace along with a few overstuffed pillows from the sofa. I set the mugs of cocoa on the brick step in front of the fireplace before sitting next to Elijah.

The flickering light from the fire illuminated the room with a warmhearted glow, giving me the feeling I was home. The two of us sat for hours by the fire, catching up on some time that we had missed with each other due to our busyness with the wedding plans. Being the day before our birthdays, and only four days before the wedding, we had had little time together lately. It was nice to have a break from the hectic schedule that we were keeping. After a while, I began to get sleepy. With the warmth from the fire and the gentleness of Elijah's arms around me, I didn't fight it, but succumbed to the sleep that claimed me. When I awoke some time later, the mantle clock read 10:30pm.

I rolled closer to Elijah, cuddling up under his outstretched arm that had held my head while I slept. I traced the lines of his tanned face with my finger, willing him to wake up. He stirred slightly, then, smiled as he drew me closer.

"What time is it?" he asked sleepily.

"It's 10:30. We should probably get home," I said reluctantly.

The rain drummed heavily on the tin roof, making me shiver.

"I'll go. You stay by the fire. I'll come back for you in the morning. I'll go over and tell your papa you'll be staying here so he won't worry. No sense in both of us getting soaked," he said firmly.

I agreed. I had no intention of getting wet while riding in the partially open buggy. I knew he would only take the horse to save time, causing him to get even more soaked. I felt sorry for him, but we both knew it wasn't proper for him to remain in the house with me over night without a chaperone.

After he left, I rested upon the sofa nearest the fire, not wanting to sleep in the master bedroom until the night of our wedding. Sleep overcame me quickly, for the day's choring had worn me out.

The rising sun seeped in through the tall windows that framed the French doors. I hadn't yet taken the time to dress them in anything but sheer curtains, so the light flowed in freely. When I roused from my deep slumber, the sun was warming me to the point that I threw off the blanket. The smell of fresh coffee reached my senses and I sat up quickly, feeling a little disoriented from sleeping in an unfamiliar place.

I craned my neck to see into the kitchen, so I could learn who was in there making the coffee. It was Elijah, just as I'd hoped. His very presence had stirred me from my sleep, and he began whistling when he saw that I was awake.

"Happy birthday, my little wild flower," he called to me from the kitchen.

"It's not—is it?"

I nearly panicked at the thought of forgetting that it was our birthday.

"Oh my, it is," I corrected myself, trying to wake up. "Happy birthday, Elijah. How in the world could I have forgotten such an important thing?"

"You have had a lot on your mind with getting the house ready and wedding preparations. I understand," he offered in comfort.

"But I didn't get ya anything. I'm so sorry,"

He hugged me and smiled.

"I have all I need right here in my arms," he claimed.

"At least let me get the coffee. Don't ya have work to do this mornin'?"

I sat up, intending to bring in the pot of coffee, but began to smooth some of the wrinkles in my long skirt instead.

"Papa gave me the day off. It's my birthday, and the birthday of my little wild flower," he said, smiling. "He could hardly expect that I'd get much work done on such an important day. I took care of the early morning chores already, so I'm yours for the entire day, if you'll have me."

I cuddled in close to keep warm against the cool morning breeze that had pushed its way in through the open fireplace flue. The fire had not been tended to since the night before and only a few embers remained.

A knock at the side door startled us both. The door opened before I got up to answer it and in walked a breathless Rachel Zook.

"Elijah, come quick. Rebekah is having her baby. *Mam* needs ya to get Doctor Beiler," Rachel managed in-between heavy breathing.

"Why doesn't she want the midwife?" Elijah asked as he threw on his jacket.

"Mam says the baby's breech."

After Elijah was out the door, she explained that she had run all the way down the path, and was struggling to speak and breathe at the same time. Elijah left Eli hitched to the buggy, which he intended to take me home in, and rode away on our new horse, Banjo, as quickly as the horse would take him. I put on a fresh pan of milk for cocoa, hoping that Rachel would have time to catch her breath before we made the treck back toward the Zook farm. The rain had turned to sleet, and we knew it would be a rough ride up the hill if it iced over.

We went straight to Mitchell's new house, where the couple had moved only one month before, to check on Rebekah. My mother informed me that she was still in the mid-stages of labor, but in a great deal of pain because of the baby's position. I knew that Elijah had worked Banjo to get to Dr. Beiler quickly because he was desperately needed.

When the sound of the horse's hooves passed through my ears, I hurried out to greet Elijah. The doctor went into the house to tend to Rebekah, while Elijah tended to both our horses and Dr. Beiler's horse. I wrapped my shawl around me to guard against the early morning air that had turned quite frigid. The rain and sleet had finally ceased, but the October storm left icy patches along the partially frozen ground.

"I suppose this means we won't be resuming our birthday celebration until later," Elijah said soberly.

"Of course not, silly. We are about to have a new niece!" I said excitedly.

"What if it turns out to be a farmer?" Elijah joked.

I poked his ribs in fun, while trying to convince him that it wouldn't happen that way. Rebekah had her heart set on having a daughter, and I thought it would be nice to hope along with her.

The morning turned to afternoon, and before long, the wind pushed heavier storm clouds along the sky. As the day wore on, the air turned colder, and the sun made itself scarce. With the clouds, came a dry dusting of snow, just light enough to dance in circles along the ground, orchestrated by the wind.

Elijah and I went in the house periodically to warm our selves. It wasn't easy listening to Rebekah cry, but I knew that each cry would bring her long-awaited baby closer to being born. Nadine and Hannah stayed in the large kitchen of their home to tidy up and keep a constant flow of fresh tea and coffee for everyone that waited. Elijah and I started walking up to the main house when Hannah suddenly opened the door to alert us that the waiting was finally over.

I knew all was well when the bright smiles of the family's faces gave away the much-awaited news. I breathed easier when I saw the beautiful baby girl, whom they named Bethany Nicole. Rebekah and Mitchell seemed like natural parents as they took turns holding her. I admired the gentleness that my brother displayed with his new daughter. He was a man who was truly in love with his family—it could be seen clearly though the glint in his eyes.

After the long day of waiting for Bethany to be born, I only wanted a hot bath and a fresh dress. I asked

Elijah to meet me at our new house at six o'clock. I had decided to make him dinner as a birthday gift, since it was too cold to picnic by the creek. I hurried home to ready myself, while he tended to the evening milking with his papa. I wanted to have plenty of time to get to my new house to prepare dinner before Elijah arrived.

For my birthday, my mother gave me the antique Dutch-Boy salt-and-pepper shakers that had belonged to her mother. She also presented me with a new teapot, which I placed on the gas stove in the kitchen that would soon be mine. I arranged the salt-and-pepper shakers on the counter along with the aluminum containers for flour, sugar, coffee and tea. Nadine and Hannah had pulled together to get me some fresh tea from Forks General Store in town. My father and Abraham supplied us with a fresh supply of hay for the barn to go along with the new milking cow, which they had brought over the day before.

I admired the things my mother gave to me, knowing how tough it was for her to part with her Dutch-Boy collection. She knew how much I had admired them since I was a tiny girl, and now they were mine to keep. I had always admired the matching cookie jar also and I hoped, perhaps, that she would give it to me on another occasion.

Someday, I might be able to pass them on to a daughter of my own.

That thought caused me to blush, and I hurried to prepare the special birthday dinner for my soon-to-be husband.

In the pantry, I found fresh apples and potatoes and a Mason jar of yellow beans. I had brought a chicken from home that Daddy had freshly butchered for me, and I put the seasoned bird in the roasting pan that Elijah's *mam* had given me. Then I lit a fire and began to peel the apples and potatoes. After I was through, I prepared a pastry crust for an apple pie. Once the pie was in the top portion of the oven, I set the potatoes on the front of the stove so they could cook slowly.

It began to get warm in the large kitchen, so I went out and sat on the porch swing with my shawl wrapped around me, to wait for Elijah to arrive. The time was only five-thirty, so I relaxed a bit, thinking over the day's events and the happiness it had brought. It was exciting that the first grandchild should have the same birthday as Elijah and me. I decided it would make it easy for everyone to remember.

When I heard the clip clop of the horse's hooves, I looked up and spotted Elijah at the top of the hill. He traveled at a steady pace to reach the small valley in which our house rested. As he moved in closer, I could see that he was dressed in a crisp, blue button-up shirt and brown, tweed trousers. I knew his *mam* had been busy sewing them for him, and I was happy to see him wearing them. As he steered the horse toward the yard, I jumped off the porch to greet him. I'd been looking forward to our first meal together in our own home. I knew it would be different once we were married, but for now this would be a special night.

☞☜

After dinner, Elijah patted his stomach and smiled at me as if to say, "Job well done". Then he stoked the fire while I washed the dishes and tidied up my kitchen. I felt so fortunate to have my own home, and this house was indeed wonderful in every way. I was grateful that we had modern plumbing, and electricity generated from a large windmill that fed directly into the laundry room, which served for the washer and dryer, the water heater and the iron. The rest of the house had no electricity. We had the use of lanterns for light, and fireplaces—two upstairs and two downstairs—to heat the house. All the windows faced the North and the South, with no direct sunlight to overheat the house in summer. This way, there was always light in all the rooms, allowing the temperature to remain stable throughout every room. The house faced due south, which I thought was a great way to design it. My husband-to-be had taken a lot of time in planning to come up with the perfect design to the well built home. As I looked outside the kitchen window, I felt grateful for the warmth against the wind and the early snowfall.

"Jane, will you come sit by the fire with me and stop fussing in that kitchen," Elijah teased.

"I'll be right there," I called from the other room.

I put down the dishtowel.

He's right. I'm fussing too much, and wasting the precious, little bit of time we have together.

When I entered the room, there was a fairly large box on the floor beside Elijah. My heart skipped a beat as I caught sight of it. I sat down as he pushed the box toward me, urging me to open it. I lifted the flap excitedly, finding newspaper inside. I looked to Elijah in confusion, so he lifted the layers of paper to reveal flowers. Several bundles of dried flowers tied with twine laid waiting for me inside. There were black-eyed-Susans, daisies, multi-colored cosmos, blue cornflowers, and several others I couldn't name.

"Oh, Elijah, these are beautiful. They look like the flowers that grow wild along the meadow."

"They are. I picked them in early September. They've been drying upside down in Papa's barn ever since," he said proudly.

"This is such a beautiful thing you've done for me. After the shawl ya made for my last birthday, I wasn't sure what you'd come up with this time. I believe ya outdid yourself, and I love ya for it."

"Would ya like me to hang them for ya?" Elijah asked.

"Yeah, I would. And I know the perfect spot. I'd like them to hang in the window above the kitchen sink. That way, I can admire them even in winter. The bright colors will brighten up my day, when all there is to look at is snow," I said excitedly.

"*Jah*. That would be the perfect place."

Elijah rose from his spot on the floor to hang the flowers. He found some small nails in the barn, and began the task. I had not yet made a covering for the kitchen window, and the flowers served as a sort of rainbow curtain. There were yellows, blues, reds and cameos—arranged in just the right order to show off God's rainbow for my pleasure.

"They'll look even more beautiful with the light comin' in through the window in the morning," I said.

"I'll bet the sunrise will make the colors look even bolder," Elijah offered.

Only a few mornings away, and I will find out. Hopefully I'll be too busy cuddling Elijah to notice.

The next few days would be filled with last minute preparations for the wedding. We decided to have the dinner and the barn dance at our new home. Since I had gotten good at square dancing due to all the recent weddings, I found I enjoyed it enough to have it for our own wedding. It would also give me another chance to hear Elijah play the banjo. He had protested when I asked him to play at our wedding, but I hadn't heard him play since my brother's wedding. We had done so much dancing at Nadine's and Hannah's weddings that he never got the chance to take a turn at it. After a great deal of prodding on my part, Elijah finally agreed to play only one song on the instrument after we had a chance to have our special, first dance together.

"We shouldn't stay long," Elijah said, interrupting my wandering thoughts. "We have a lot to do in the next few days."

I knew he was right, but it didn't make things any easier. We sat by the fire a few more minutes and kissed, while discussing plans for our future. Eventually, the fire began to die down, and it was time to go back to my small space at my parent's house. It was tough to leave, knowing this was my home, and I momentarily wondered if Elijah should have waited until this day to present me with it. Though it might have made the waiting easier, I realized I would not have wanted to miss the time we had spent together at the house, preparing to make it our home.

Elijah took a ladle of water from the galvanized pail beside the fireplace and doused the remaining coals. He was tired and in need of sleep—he would have chores in only a few short hours, and the trip home would be too cold to bear if we waited any longer.

TEN
A TIME TO LOVE

October was already earning its reputation for being one of the coldest fall months—one of the reasons we decided not to wait until November to wed. As silly as my mother had thought it to be, I didn't want to have to wear a jacket with my wedding dress. I felt the dress itself was plenty heavy enough for fall, but not quite enough for a cold winter month.

ಶೋೕಚಿ

The following two days were spent in preparation for the wedding, allowing very little time for Elijah and me to spend time with one another. It was good that we kept busy, or I may have been too tempted to spend the time with him and slack off my duties. There was so much work to be done; it was easy to become overwhelmed by it all. I didn't care as much about the wedding as I was concerned about being a wife. I already felt like his wife in every way except one, and that would change at the end of my wedding day.

ಬಿಂಬ

The day of my wedding finally arrived and I was up at five in the morning. I was obviously more nervous than I ever thought I could be. It didn't really make sense to me that I should be nervous. After all, I was to wed the man for whom I'd been waiting for a long time. Maybe it was the thought of the wedding night that I couldn't seem to shake from my nerves. Deborah and Miriam would be over soon, but I only wanted Nadine's company. I needed to talk to my sister, much in the same way we had before she married Benjamin.

Without warning, a knock came at the door. It was Nadine, and she opened the door before I could invite her in.

"Boy, am I glad to see you!"

"I saw from my house that your lamp was lit, so I thought I'd come over and see why ya couldn't sleep," my sister whispered.

"Well, how come you're up this early?" I asked.

"I suppose I had the jitters for ya, and decided to get up and pray."

"I sure could use a sister talk right now. I must confess; I'm a bit worried about—well—tonight."

She looked a little lost at my statement so I began to clarify my meaning, making sure I was cautious about my wording.

"Don't worry little sister; it'll be a new experience for both of ya. God'll make it right for ya since ya both honored his commands," she tried to reassure me.

"But I feel nervous and shy about him seein' me without my dress. How on earth did ya manage to get through it?" I asked nervously.

"You'll be married. That's the way God intended for married people to be on their wedding night. Adam and Eve were naked in the garden. She was his wife, and God didn't let her have clothing. Adam was her husband," she explained.

"Can ya pray with me about it?" I asked.

"Of course I will," she comforted me.

We sat on my bed and held hands as she began a sweet and sincere prayer on my behalf.

"Lord God, we come before your throne to thank ya for this very special day. Be with Jane on her weddin' night, and bless her with courage and self-esteem so she'll be able to reap the reward of stayin' pure accordin' to your word. Bless Elijah with gentleness and patience if needed, for this very special time for them as a married couple. In Jesus name, Amen."

"Amen," I whispered.

We sat on the bed for a minute, tears running down our cheeks. I hugged my sister and told her how much she meant to me. I knew I would be fine—God would be with me to comfort my fears about my wedding night with Elijah.

ഇരുന്നു

The strong smell of coffee let us know that we were no longer the only family members awake. It was confirmed when Miriam entered my room with a smile of anticipation.

"Are ya ready for your big day?" Miriam asked.

"I am now," I said as I gave Nadine one last squeeze.

I wiped away the last of my tears, determined to cry only happy tears for the rest of my life.

Nadine excused herself so she could go home to prepare her husband's breakfast. Deborah then showed up with the bouquets she had assembled from some of the fancier, late-blooming wildflowers from her family's flower patch. They were beautiful and full of color—just the way I had requested. Across the room, my full wedding gown hung form a peg on the wall. It was simple, but trimmed with lace, with a full flowing train that Molly, as the flower girl, would carry down the aisle of the church. Our ceremony would be more of a traditional one, with very little Amish customs. I had requested it that way, and Elijah had allowed me the indulgence of such.

After a hot bath and a cup of coffee, I was ready for Miriam and Deborah to help me get the long wedding gown and the things needed to fix my hair into the waiting buggy.

By the time we reached the Mennonite Church, it was filled with family and friends in the community. I went into a side room where my mother and my attendants assisted me with my dress and hair. My veil consisted of a flowered ring that went around my hair, with a trail of lacy material hanging down from the back.

My hands grew shaky as the time drew near for the ceremony. I couldn't quite figure out why I felt such nervousness, but I knew it didn't have anything to do with my feelings toward Elijah. I believe the prospect of going through such a private thing in front of so many people made my stomach churn a bit. I felt fortunate that I had not eaten any breakfast, fearing that it might come back up. At the same time, I was hungry and in need of something. My mother handed me a cup of tea, as though she knew what I was thinking. The tea was just what I needed to settle my stomach, making me less fidgety.

My father entered the already overcrowded room to inform me that everyone was ready. It was a good thing for me because if I had had to wait much longer, I may have become more agitated. Miriam and Deborah left to take their positions in the hall to walk the aisle before me.

When we were alone, my father turned to me and spoke; his eyes full of fresh tears that threatened to spill over.

"I love ya Jane. I may not have always been there for ya when you were dealing with the things your mother did, and I'm plenty sorry for it. But I'm here for ya now, and I always will be if ya need me," he said, still teary-eyed.

"Did Nadine get this talk too, Daddy?" I asked jokingly.

He smiled, making the air seem a little lighter between us.

"Am I goin' a little overboard," he asked.

Nah. I'm glad you're my daddy. I love ya, and I'd never change that, not for anything in the world," I said, trying to hold back the tears.

If the truth be told, it hadn't been easy being his daughter. Or having such a painful past. Or being a member of my family. Although I knew that it was not something I could share with him yet, he seemingly was offering me the chance to expose the sorrow from the abuse that I had suffered only a few short years ago.

Fortunately, the hardest part of my life was finally over—the growing up part. And I'd forgiven him for not being there to save me from the abuse my mamma had put me through. It was now time to put my childhood behind me and go forward. It no longer mattered that he was never around to spare me the hurt that my mother had put on me—he turned out to be a good father, and that changed everything—just as Mamma's salvation had.

Suddenly, for the first time in my life, I no longer felt afraid of what the future would hold for me. I knew what God's immediate plan for my life was, and I felt I had a lot to look forward to. After a short silence, my father spoke softly, letting me know that the moment of truth had arrived.

"Well let's go honey," he urged. "Elijah's been waitin' a long time for ya. We mustn't let him wait another minute."

"Just one more thing, Daddy. I want to tell you one more thing."

"What's that, Jane?"

"Thanks for movin' us here, Daddy."

I put on a smile and took a deep breath as we exited the little room to take our place at the back of the church.

I looked out at the crowd that had gathered to witness our special day.

Well, this is it. I'm a grown woman now, and I'm about to be a wife.

The large, pipe organ sounded the signal for the ceremony to begin. First, Deborah and Matthew walked down the aisle, followed by Miriam and Jonathon. I took another deep breath as the organist cued my descent toward the front of the church and my eager husband-to-be. Elijah's eyes caught mine as I left the foyer and made my way down the aisle. The look in his eyes was one of pure love—for me. I felt like the luckiest woman in the world as I took my place beside Elijah at the altar.

In my nervous state, I struggled to concentrate on the words being said by the preacher.

"In the consummation of the first marriage between Adam and Eve: the woman, whom God has made as a helper for man, was not taken from his head to rule over him, nor from his feet as to be trampled by him—but from his side that she might be his equal. From under his arm, that she might receive his protection. And from near his heart, that she might own and command his love," the words flowed freely from his tongue to our ears.

The ceremony went quicker than I'd imagined it to. Still, it was lovely. When given our cue, Elijah and I kissed a lengthy kiss that didn't go unnoticed by the crowd of family and friends in attendance. Suddenly lost in that kiss, I felt the gentle nudge from the preacher to cease. When we finally separated from one another, there was a gentle hush of laughter from the spectators. My face turned several shades of red—so much that I didn't dare face the multitude that watched. Elijah and I locked eyes for a brief moment before the preacher announced our status as a wedded couple. I thought I detected a glimmer of tears in his eyes.

"May I present Mr. and Mrs. Elijah Zook," he announced.

Keeping my face toward the ground, I swallowed hard the lump in my throat, trying not to alert anyone to my still-nervous state. Once we exited the church, we were free to leave. Elijah assisted me into the buggy, then climbed aboard and clicked to Eli, prompting him to begin a slow trot.

"Why are we goin' the opposite way?" I asked Elijah. "They'll be expectin' us at the house for dinner."

"I thought we'd take a little detour before we greet our friends and family at the house. Is that all right with you my beautiful wife?"

His words caught me by surprise, but I enjoyed the sound of it.

"Say it again," I urged him.

"I love you, Mrs. Zook," he said boastfully.

I grinned widely at his declaration of love for me, for he had finally become my husband. After all the waiting, I suddenly felt a peaceful warmth come over me, strong enough to take away the chill in the air. I snuggled in closer to Elijah, enough to get under his waiting arm. I knew without a doubt that it was there that I was meant to be.

Elijah suddenly halted the horse, then, turned to me with a smile. He kissed me gently on the lips, making me want more from him than what he offered. It comforted me to know that we would never again have to stop ourselves in the passionate love that we had for one another. I also knew that this was not the time for any of that, married or not. We were already risking a lot, as the Amish did not show affection in public—newlywed or not, and I knew the rules. After all, the kiss at the church was far longer than was expected by all that observed it.

"I didn't bring ya here to get all involved with kissing and the like. I wanted to have you to myself for a few minutes before everyone took your attention from me for the rest of the day. I wanted a minute to look at my beautiful bride. After today, you'll be my wife—only today will ya be my bride. I just want to remember everything about this day."

His voice poured forth all the love that I had been waiting to share with him ever since I first laid my eyes on him. He kissed me again, and I gave in to his irresistible charm. Knowing that we had our wedding night ahead of us made it easier to stop when Elijah prompted.

"Shall we ride back and fulfill our duty to our families?"

"I suppose we ought to get back," I agreed reluctantly.

"We have the rest of our lives to be together. This is our family's time, and we would be selfish if we didn't allow them their time. Don't mistake my words. I want so much to jump ahead to our time alone tonight. However, I love ya so much it will be worth the wait. That is what has made me strong enough to wait for our wedding night—and God's strength, of course," he said, laughing lightheartedly.

He was so wise—one of the many reasons I admired him so. With one click from Elijah, Eli was trotting along the path that led to our new home. As we approached the hill, we looked down at our property, which was already filled with buggies and people—all of them eagerly awaiting our arrival. We both took a deep breath as we made our way down the trail that led to the celebration. Family members followed us into the house as we entered to partake in the wedding banquet.

Elijah seated me at the main table, then, took his place at my right, as is proper seating at Amish wedding dinners. The Miller family did the serving for the day, and even kept up with the cleaning. I had to admit that I was worried at first, regarding the amount of people that had squeezed into our home. The respect for our things was overwhelmingly taken into consideration, and I felt confident that by the day's end, all would be back in its place in our large home.

80C8

It seemed a small eternity before the last guests bid their good wishes and good-byes to us. Even though the hour had only reached eight o'clock, I felt wiped out from the day's events. I wondered how I would muster up enough energy to spend the remainder of the evening with my new husband in solitude. I was grateful that Nadine and Benjamin had assisted the move of our personal belongings into the house the day before, for it gave me a sense that the house was finally my own.

Once inside my new bedroom, I removed Elijah's Bible from his bedside table and took it into the bathroom with me as I readied myself for my husband. I held the Bible in my hands as I traced over the raised gold lettering that read; King James.

I lit the lantern and laid aside my bedclothes. Then I sat on the edge of the bathtub to read as I turned on the water to fill the large tub. I felt the need for a hot soak before retiring, due to the heavy load I had endured throughout the week. I felt weary and even a bit scared, yet giddy as I prayed for God's guidance to a scripture that would prepare me for my time alone with Elijah. Nadine had suggested reading The Song of Solomon, but I still felt the need to pray for guidance.

Before I realized, I had opened my husband's Bible to the very pages my sister had suggested. I scrolled through for several minutes before deciding to fetch my own version from my bedside table. I compared the two until my bath was filled. Then, I settled into the tub, placing my Bible aside. I didn't need to read the verses anymore; I'd read them so many times already I had them mostly memorized.

Let him kiss me with the kisses of his mouth—for your love is more delightful than wine. Pleasing is the fragrance of your perfumes; your name is like perfume poured out.... My lover is to me a sachet of myrrh resting between my breasts.... How handsome you are, my lover! Oh, how charming! And our bed is verdant.... My lover is mine and I am his; he browses among the lilies. Until the day breaks and the shadows flee.... Do not arouse or awaken love until it so desires....

I glanced over at the closed Bible, intending to let the evening unfold as God designed it to. Then I said a quick prayer for wisdom as I heard Elijah enter the bedroom.

When a knock came at the bathroom door, I sat up, pulling my knees to my chest, and instinctively covering my breasts with crossed arms. My fear took over me, not allowing me to answer the knock. After a short pause, the door opened and my husband entered the dimly lit room. He was still dressed in his suit from the wedding, and I felt exposed in total nakedness.

He looks so handsome. But what will he think of me? Please don't look at me yet, I'm not ready.

He knelt down beside the tub without saying a word to me, and dipped his hand in the water to retrieve the sea sponge that I used when I bathed. He squeezed the sponge over my shoulders, allowing the warm water to drip across my breasts, which I still protected from his sight. I felt somewhat vulnerable in my nakedness—much in the same way that I had as a child. Throughout most of my childhood, my mother had repeatedly told me that my body was dirty, and it was to be kept covered. Even now it was difficult to shake the lies that I had grown up believing. I knew I was allowed to be naked in my husband's presence, as Adam and Eve had been in the Garden of Eden. However, I lacked the knowledge of how to react to Elijah's boldness.

Oh Lord, give me the courage to let go of my breasts, I prayed in my mind.

Elijah didn't pressure me—he handled my feelings with a quiet gentleness. Soon, I felt kisses on the back of my neck and shoulders as he continued to sponge water across my back. My face turned to his, allowing him to kiss my lips. Being lost in my love for him, I began to relax, forgetting about my nakedness. He stopped kissing me and looked into my eyes, then pulled two gold rings from his pant pocket and held them in his open hand. I instinctively took the larger one from his hand without saying a word and placed it on his finger. He placed the other ring on my finger, then, stood to his feet and reached for my over-sized bath towel. I stood to meet him as he wrapped the towel around me. Then he lifted me gently from the tub and carried me to our bed where I gave myself to him.

෨෬

In the morning, I woke later than normal. The sun was up, but my new husband was not beside me. I remembered stirring several hours before, when he had risen to milk the cows.

I rolled over and reached for my absent husband, longing to be near him. As I did, I remembered a line in the scripture I had read in Elijah's Bible the night before.

I sought him whom my soul loveth: I sought him, but I found him not.

Elijah's pillow didn't comfort me any, but I cradled it nonetheless. I held up my hand and admired the ring that Elijah had placed on my finger as evidence that I was his.

The wearing of wedding rings was forbidden in the Amish community, but my husband had given in to my desire to have them and I loved him even more for it.

I fluffed Elijah's pillow under me and thought how good it felt to finally be a wife. I felt so different—grown up—in a way that I wasn't sure I fully understood yet. I no longer felt as an innocent child, for I had been transformed to a woman through a Godly union with my husband. Without a moment's thought, I determined that it had definitely been well worth the wait.

The following is a sneak peek of the continuing story of Jane and Elijah in Book Two...

LITTLE WILD FLOWER

Book Two

ONE
AS TIME GOES BY

The first few weeks of marriage were filled with fun and adjustments. Even though I had been a big help at home for my mother with cooking and the taking care of Sammy, I hadn't had to do any of it full time for a few years. After previously being the total caregiver when my mother had been so sick from the alcohol she couldn't care for my younger siblings, I sometimes found it to be habit to want to take over. But before I moved away from home, I had settled into a good routine with her. We had begun to work well together.

Nadine, for the most part, had handled all the laundry at home until she married Benjamin. My mother took over that chore once Nadine moved out, and I had merely assisted her up until then. Though she'd been well enough to handle the daily routine on her own for some time, it was still difficult for me to let go and accept that my mother had healed from the scars of the past. Truth be told, though I loved my new role as a wife to Elijah, it was hard for me to break free from the role as caregiver to my mother, even if I was just down the lane from her, I felt the separation from her stronger than I ever thought I would. I'd begun to depend on her as a mother and a friend—a friend I would now need as I grew apart from her to settle into my own new routine as the wife of an Amish farmer.

Now, it seemed, while Elijah tended to our new herd of cattle, I was very busy cooking and cleaning. Doing the laundry and chores at my own house; including feeding the chickens and gathering eggs, proved to be full time work for me. I never imagined just how rewarding it could feel to accomplish these things until it was for the sake of my own home and my own husband.

Just when I began to get myself into a routine; my body, it would seem, decided to rebel. I began to get sick every morning, throwing my schedule into a whirlwind. One crisp morning at the end of November, Mitchell and Benjamin showed up at the house to assist Elijah with adding more fencing around our property to accommodate the increasing herd. Nadine and Rebekah tagged along, with little Bethany in tow, hoping we could share the afternoon meal together once the men's work was done.

Nadine had brought some sausage to cook potato soup, and the very sight of the raw meat was making me feel nauseated. The smells of food cooking in the kitchen had recently become too much for me to handle. My husband had eaten oatmeal and cornmeal for the last several mornings so I could cut down on cooking smells. I hadn't planned on having my queasy stomach interrupt any more of my time, but it seemed very determined to hang around a little longer. I had hoped it would pass before

Rebekah brought the baby over because I feared passing the flu to her.

"You look a little green around the gills, Jane," Nadine joked.

She placed the sausage in the hot skillet, sending a sizzling burst of smell straight to my nostrils.

"I think I may have the flu or somethin'. I've been awful sick for the last four days, 'cept I don't have a fever, and I haven't thrown up yet," I said.

I held a hand over my nose to keep from inhaling too much of the aroma from the sizzling sausage.

"Are ya sick all day, or just in the morning?" Rebekah asked.

"Mostly in the mornin'. How did ya know that?"

I sat in one of the kitchen chairs, hoping to keep from toppling over from the wave of nausea that was trying very hard to overcome me.

She hesitated, watching as I fought the urge to run from the room to empty my stomach.

"You might be pregnant."

"Come to think of it, I haven't had my cycle since two weeks before the wedding."

The reality of what she said had time enough to sink in.

"I'll bet it happened on your wedding night, then. How romantic that is," Rebekah said.

"Do ya think I could be pregnant, really?"

I felt excitement and fear at the same time.

"Maybe we should get mamma to take ya into town to see Doctor Beiler," Nadine suggested.

"Should I say somethin' to Elijah about it?"

"Ya can if ya want to, but maybe ya ought to wait until ya see the doctor. It's always best if ya see the doctor for your first pregnancy, especially since ya don't know for sure," Rebekah said.

Bethany began to fuss, so Rebekah went to change her.

"Gosh, Jane. I'm gonna be jealous if ya have a baby before me," Nadine said.

"I'm not so sure there's anything to be jealous about. This whole thing is makin' me nervous."

"You're right, Jane. We should wait until ya hear it from Doc Beiler anyway."

ഏറ

Two days later, my mother drove me into town to see the doctor. He confirmed that I was indeed six weeks pregnant after doing a thorough exam.

Thoroughly embarrassing was more like it.

I was excited but scared, but I also couldn't wait to share the news with my husband.

After our stop at the doctor's office, my mother and I did a little shopping for yard goods for making baby clothes and maternity dresses. I knew I had my work cut out for me, but I also knew that I could count on my sister and Hannah to help.

That evening after dinner, Elijah and I sat by the fire discussing our plans for our first Christmas together as husband and wife.

"I thought you might like to have the family get-together at our house, since it will be our first Christmas in our new home. I'm sure both our sisters and our mothers would be very helpful to you if you wanted the help," he offered.

"It sounds like a wonderful idea," I said with excitement at the idea of entertaining in my new house.

The non-stop smile on my face was due more to the news that I had for my husband, and I was afraid I was going to give it away before I could tell him.

"What are you so happy about?" he asked me.

"We are having a baby," I blurted out.

He flashed me a look of uncertainty.

Not the reaction I'd hoped for.

"I went to see the doctor today," I tried again. "He said I am pregnant,"

Elijah jumped up from the floor and let out a whoop. I stood up and laughed at his excitement. Before I could gain my composure, he picked me up and swung me around the room. Tears filled his eyes and we both laughed and cried for several minutes.

"I love you so much," he declared.

That's more like it.

"I love you too. But would ya put me down—I'm getting a little queasy," I begged good-naturedly.

He set me down and we sat by the fire holding each other until we fell asleep.

ౠౚ

The Christmas season swept in around the town-folk like a magical force; causing winter merriment to spread like the snowflakes that collected on the roof-tops and tree branches. The snow; thankfully, was not too deep yet to keep our family from celebrating together as we always had. Elijah and I decided we would wait to tell the rest of the family the news of my pregnancy until our family dinner together at our house.

I prepared dinner with a nervous excitement, wondering about the reactions of my in-laws to our news. I wanted more than anything to see a look of acceptance on the face of Elijah's *mam*. Not even since the wedding had I felt she truly accepted me as the right one for her first-born son. She'd always been pleasant, and I knew she loved me in some sort of sense, but I strongly needed her approval for my own peace of mind. Elijah and I had had many a discussion over his mother's guarded nature where I was concerned, but thankfully, she never interfered.

As the announcement was made over dinner, Elijah's voice was steady, unlike my own would have been. I was proud to be by his side, my hand clenching his for support and reassurance.

The reaction was almost overwhelming. Everyone was happy for us and cheered loudly. I looked over at Naomi, wondering what she was thinking. As we made eye contact, her eyes were brimming with tears that threatened to spill from her smiling eyes.

God, please let those be happy tears falling from my new *mam's* eyes.

Before I could think another thought, David stood up and began to clear his throat to get everyone's attention.

"If it's announcements we're making, Hannah and I are expecting our first child too," he said proudly.

Everyone cheered until Mitchell stood up.

"Now that's not fair. Rebekah and I didn't get this much attention when we announced her pregnancy at Thanksgiving. Just b'cause this is our second baby, doesn't mean ya can't all cheer for us too. C'mon now, I'm waitin'," he joked.

The entire crowd of family and friends roared with laughter and cheers to the point of embarrassment for poor Rebekah. I guess she hadn't realized until that moment what a ham my brother could be. I did wonder, though, how Rebekah would handle being pregnant again so soon after having Bethany. After all, Bethany would only be eleven months old when the new one came along.

We continued to laugh heartily until an unfamiliar sound swept through the air. I strained my ears to figure out the sound, looking for Elijah for an explanation, but he had managed to slip away unnoticed. I followed the jingling sound that was ringing in my ears, while looking around corners for my husband. The magnificent sound was coming from the front of the house, so I opened the front door. Much to my surprise, I saw Elijah in a sleigh with Eli and Banjo hitched to it.

"Merry Christmas," Elijah hollered cheerfully.

He held out his arms toward the sleigh, motioning me to come to him. My mother handed me my heavy coat and assisted me in pulling on my boots, then, urged me to join my husband. I walked carefully onto the porch so I wouldn't slip on the fresh layer of snow that had blown onto it. Elijah walked up the steps to help me down to where the sleigh was waiting for us. The impatient horses blew rolling puffs of icy air from their nostrils that glistened against the blue light of the moon.

"Is this for me?" I asked excitedly.

"It is for you, my little wild flower," he said lovingly as he bowed slightly.

A boyish grin spread wide across his face. "May I have the pleasure of my beautiful wife's company for a moonlit sleigh ride?"

I played along and offered him my hand. "You may."

He took my hand and assisted me into the sleigh, then sat down close beside me. Then he placed heavy woolen blankets around our laps, and clicked a command to the horses. I looked to the front porch where my family eagerly waved us off. They appeared to be just as excited as I was by the surprise gift.

As we pulled away from the house, the horses started out walking slowly, while the bells provided a gentle chiming, but when they began a slow trot, the bells jingled a steady, romantic rhythm. I looked into Elijah's eyes excitedly, allowing the love that he had for me to keep me warm.

ಹಿ‍ೞ

As the ice began to melt from the creek bank, crocuses pushed their way through the light layer of snow that remained in patches along the warming soil. The smell of fresh soil made me eager to make plans for the oversized patch of earth that was to become my own garden. My mind skipped ahead to canning season, wondering which vegetables I would like to have and which ones might be easier to grow. Having very little luck with my first garden at my mother's house, I was already aware of what I was capable of growing without much effort. But this was different. This would provide food for my husband; and for that reason alone, I made up my mind to challenge myself.

I went to my father, knowing he would have plenty of seeds from the previous season. Even if he lacked some seeds, Abraham's collection would be there to fill in the gaps. Just as I'd suspected, my father's assortment of seeds in the barn was overwhelming. All carefully labeled, the small paper sacks that housed the seeds invited me to explore so many possibilities in my mind's eye.

My father watched as I pored over the selection of seeds with excitement.

"Ya don't need to have an entire field your first season."

"I know, Papa. But Elijah will be countin' on me to help feed the family."

I patted my swelling abdomen lovingly.

"Elijah will provide for ya, Jane. Did ya forget ya married an experienced farmer?"

"How could I forget a thing like that? Why do ya think I'm so determined to have the best garden I can?"

He smiled knowingly, then, helped me sift through my increasing mixture of vegetable and flower seeds. There was no changing my mind once it was made it up, and he knew me well enough to allow my stubbornness to rule me.

⁝ϫϳ

The heat of July swept across Indiana with full force, making the last four weeks of my pregnancy nearly unbearable. Lucy had come to stay with me so Elijah could keep up with the chores around the farm without having to tend to my every need as well. Lucy and I sat on the porch swing sipping lemonade, allowing the subtle breeze to dry the perspiration from our foreheads. The fragrant blossoms from the lilac bushes that surrounded the porch perfumed the air as the breeze drifted along lazily.

We had fed the chickens earlier and had intended on weeding a bit in the garden, but it quickly became too hot and humid. We decided to tend to the garden after the dinner hour, just before the mosquitoes would become a nuisance. For now, we shelled some of the early peas from my garden into the new colander Elijah purchased from Forks General Store when he had gone into town the day before. My own trips to town had been curtailed about a month prior, due to my increasing girth. The heaviness of the child within me rested too heavily upon my bladder, making the jostling from the buggy too painful for me to bear.

I took off my shoes and long knit stockings to relieve myself somewhat of the heat. The increasing girth of my pregnancy made it a difficult task, but I was determined to get free from the sweltering heat that my stockings held in. The wind floated up the skirting of my dress, giving me some relief, but I decided I wanted to wade in the creek. As Lucy helped me to my feet, we both laughed at the difficulty I had in getting up from the swing.

The thick grass cooled my tired feet as we walked along the worn path that was partially covered with grass. Nadine met us at the fork of the path that led from her home. She too, was too warm in her last term of her pregnancy, and wanted to wade the creek with us. Nadine's pregnancy was nearly three months behind my own, which amazed all of us, since it was the first pregnancy for both of us. Benjamin and Nadine had waited a while to start their family, but Elijah and I had not planned it that way. We knew that whenever God chose to bless us, we would become parents, and we were blessed with news of my pregnancy less than two months after we were wed. It had been a time of great adjustment for me. To be newly pregnant and newlywed at the same time proved stressful in the beginning. However, I soon learned to adjust with the help of an understanding husband.

Mitchell and Rebekah, on the other hand, had recently had their second child—a boy, whom they named Jordan. And though he was born early, there were no complications. I didn't intend to have my children that close together. In fact, as tough as being pregnant was on a body, I wasn't certain I would agree to have any more than the one I already carried.

Life in the Amish community was rough on most of the women, but I was fortunate that my husband had allowed for a modern electric washer and dryer. Without them, I may not have gotten through our first winter too easily. I enjoyed hanging clothes on the outside line if the weather permitted, but I wouldn't have given up that dryer for most anything, especially since I was pregnant. I didn't mind using the gas stove in which to cook, or the lanterns for light, but I sure was happy that Elijah had the generosity in his heart to allow me the luxury of a water heater to heat my bath water. Having the use of electricity in our laundry room cut down on a lot of stress for me in my pregnant state. Our windmill generated the electricity, and although I couldn't quite grasp the engineering of it from Elijah's explanations, I knew it worked, and that was all that mattered to me.

The creek was almost bitter cold, which caused my feet to throb. Still, it was refreshing in small jaunts. For nearly an hour, we walked in and out of the water, laughing and splashing until we were nearly soaked. We sat on the bank to dry in the sun, discussing names for our babies, while Lucy interjected with some strange suggestions of her own.

Hannah joined us, and we all sat around discussing names, much to the bore of poor Lucy. We didn't intend to exclude her, but she was the only one of us that was not expecting a child. Hannah and I were due on the same day, but she looked as though she were about to give birth any day, whereas I expected to be pregnant for another month. Hannah was determined that she would only have girls, and she had already decided on the names Rachel and Ezra for them, claiming that David, her husband, had given her full reign over naming them if her children were to be girls.

This excited Hannah, therefore, we continued to throw different, and, some unusual names around.

After a while, Lucy became somewhat anxious, and went up to the house to fetch a pail to pick berries with. Hannah watched her curiously as she walked along the path, waiting for her to be out of earshot before she spoke to me.

"Jane, why is it that Lucy stays with ya, and not Rachel?"

"My sister or Elijah's? We have two Rachel's, remember?" I asked her.

"I meant *your* sister. She doesn't seem that close to any of you girls. How come?" she asked with curious caution in her tone.

"Well, that's a long story. B'fore we moved here, we weren't exactly raised to be that close. Nadine and I always got along pretty good, but the two of us and Mitchell were so much older when the rest of the kids came along, that it seemed as though they were part of another family," I tried explaining.

"But that still doesn't explain why you have such a *gut* time with Lucy. She's even younger than Rachel."

"Lucy is an exception. When she was a baby, I took on a lot of her care—almost like she was my own child. My *mam* was ill for a while, so I kinda took over bein' the mamma for a while. Nadine did some of the housework with me, so I mostly played mamma to the younger ones. Rachel was old enough at that time that she took care of herself. She's kinda kept to herself ever since."

"She's a lot more social with us now than she was b'fore we came here," Nadine interjected. "But I don't think she'll ever wanna be part of regular family stuff."

"That's a special thing ya got with Lucy, you know it Jane?"

She wasn't asking, she was telling me how it was, and I didn't have any problem accepting it as truth. I would have liked it more if I had had a close relationship with all my siblings, but it hadn't turned out that way. I knew I couldn't have any regrets though, or I would have no reason to appreciate the love that our family had found after moving to the farmhouse.

The sun rested high in the sky, alerting us to the fact that we would be needed at home to prepare the noon meal for our hard-working husbands. After kicking along the creek for another few minutes, we started walking toward home where plenty of work awaited us.

∞∞

On the twentieth day of July, I awoke to the feeling of a delightful twinge in my abdomen, alerting me to the fact that the birth of my first child was eminent. The awareness that I had of my surroundings became dulled when a sharp pain quivered across my back. I hadn't even realized that I was standing in a puddle of water on the bathroom floor. When I felt the gentle trickle of warm water on my legs, I knew then that my water had broken. I tried in desperation to blot the seemingly never-ending flow of water, while I called nervously for my husband.

"Elijah, where are you?" I begged desperately for his whereabouts.

Holding a towel around me, I walked to the French doors that led to our balcony leading out to the back of the house. I yelled once more for my husband, who seemed to be nowhere in the general area. Panic ran through me before I had the chance to gather my thoughts and breathe a short prayer.

"Oh Lord, help me not to be afraid of the unknown. Help me to stay calm until my husband returns from his morning chores. Please bless this child that is within me, and give me the strength to endure the pain that is to come."

Just then, I heard Nadine calling to me from my bedroom door.

"Hey sweetie, are ya up yet? I let myself in because ya didn't answer the door."

Her voice was cheerful.

"In here." I answered, relieved not to be alone anymore. I pulled my robe around me and turned on the water to fill the oversized tub.

"Where's Lucy," she called from the other room before finding me in the bathroom.

"She must be in the hen house. She didn't hear me when I called for Elijah."

She smiled at me, until she studied my pale face.

"Are ya okay?" she asked as she grabbed my arm to steady me.

"I'm havin' another big contraction," I said breathlessly.

"How long have ya been havin' them?"

"Well, that depends. I've been feelin' achy for about three hours, but I've been layin' in the bed strugglin' to get up. It only started feelin' like contractions since I got outta bed about ten minutes ago," I recalled.

"Did your water break?" she asked pointing to the towel that I had wrapped around my legs.

"Yes. I was gonna take a warm bath to ease the pain in my back. Will ya sit with me?"

"Ya can't take a bath if your water broke. Ya better take a shower." She reached down and turned off the water.

"Why can't I take a bath?"

"*Mam* told me when she was havin' Molly before we moved here. Her water broke and I helped her get in the shower b'cause Dr. Dana told her not to bathe 'cause it could cause an infection in the uterus." She explained.

"I never heard of such a thing—of course with Dr. Dana, it coulda been an "old wives tale" that he told mamma. Just in case it's true though, it's a good thing ya showed up when ya did, or I might've made a big mistake."

Nadine pulled the plug to drain the tub, then, started the shower for me. The hot water soothed my back pain, allowing me to relax through the contractions. They began to come at increasingly longer lengths with fewer breaks in between. This alarmed Nadine, so she offered to get Lucy to fetch the midwife for me.

"No!" I snapped. "I want Dr. Beiler." I said with fear in my voice.

"Ya haven't even started havin' hard labor yet, so we got plenty of time to get the doctor. Put a fresh nightgown on and rest on the bed while I have Lucy round up Elijah for ya. Meanwhile, I'll go up to mom's and have her call the doc for ya. Stay calm, ya aren't even half-way there yet," she said with a smirk.

I did as she said and tried my best to remain calm. I knew the pains weren't anywhere near the intensity that I had witnessed in Naomi the night that she gave birth to Elijah's twin sisters, or with mamma's or Rebekah's labor. With that in mind, I was grateful that I had not begun to be in that much pain yet.

Elijah sent Lucy in the house to sit with me, then, showered downstairs in the mud-room to get the earth off of him so he could be of assistance. My mother and Nadine arrived with the news that Dr. Beiler was on his way. As my mother questioned me about the contractions, she took a mental note and assured me that I still had plenty of time before the baby would arrive.

Although the contractions were not increasing in intensity, I was beginning to feel more uncomfortable with each one. My mother even told me I was getting crabby.

"You should save that for the last stage of labor, honey. Most women don't get crabby until they're ready to push," she informed me.

"I do feel kinda like I could push right now," I said, wincing.

"There is *no* way you need to push now. You haven't even had any hard contractions yet. You've barely had to do any breathing through them," she said.

I grunted a little, and she warned me to stop before I wore myself out. I pushed a little more quietly, and slowly, causing the urge to push to increase. My mother and Nadine left the room to gather together some fresh towels when Elijah entered the room. I pulled him closer so she wouldn't hear me talking to him.

"I don't know if my mamma is right, but I really do feel like I gotta push. Maybe somethin's wrong," I alerted him.

"When Dr. Beiler last saw ya, didn't he say that ya shouldn't push until the baby's head is coming out?" he asked.

"I don't remember. It does sorta feel like the baby is comin' out though," I said in a grunting voice. "I think I'm havin' the baby now!"

Just then my mother came back in the room, and Elijah relayed to her what my concern was. She assured him that it wasn't time to push yet, and went about setting up the room with Nadine for the new arrival.

"Mamma, please. I think I'm havin' the baby *now*," I grunted.

"You aren't still trying to push are you?" she asked with concern.

"Mamma, it's time, I just know it," I cried. "I'm havin' the baby *now*,"

"Oh, you are not," she teased.

She walked over to the bed to check my progress, and gasped when she realized I had been right.

"Oh no! You *are* having the baby!"

"I am?"

I momentarily panicked, feeling like I could faint, but I didn't want to miss one single thing. The concern of not having a doctor present seemed to agitate Elijah.

"Shouldn't we wait for the doctor to come?" he asked my mother nervously.

"There isn't time," she stated matter-of-factly. "Babies have a way of showing up when they are good and ready, and this one is ready just like its mamma said."

Elijah got behind me as my mother instructed him to, then she took over telling me when and how long to push. When a tiny head emerged, I began to laugh as tears poured from my eyes in amazement. One more long push revealed a calm baby boy.

"Shouldn't he be cryin' or somethin' Mamma?" I asked nervously.

She turned the baby around so I could get a better look at his face. His eyes were wide open, and he appeared to be looking at his surroundings with the most gentle of dispositions I'd ever seen in a baby.

"He's so beautiful!"

I was so happy that I was crying and laughing at the same time. I turned to my husband, whose face was also filled with joyful tears, and spoke gently to him.

"With your permission, I'd like to name him Eli," I said.

Elijah gasped.

"Ya want to name him after my horse?" he asked.

"No, silly! I wanna name him after his papa. Ya told me yourself that Eli was short for Elijah," I said, smiling. "Didn't ya tell me a long time ago that ya had a great grandfather named Eli? We can't name him Elijah—that would be too confusin' to have more than one Elijah in the house, don't you think?"

"I suppose ya could be right about that. Eli it is," he said cheerfully.

My mother tied up the cord, and she let Elijah cut between the two ties. Then Nadine took our new baby boy to clean him up a little. In the excitement, I had forgotten that she was still in the room.

"This sure is a handsome boy ya got here," she said over her shoulder. "I only hope my labor goes as quickly as this one did."

My father and Doctor Beiler showed up then, and Abraham and Naomi Zook arrived in time to see their new grandchild. My parents, and the Zook's, seemed to be very proud of their new grandson, but I still felt nervous having my in-laws seemingly inspecting my child. I wanted privacy with my husband so we could admire our baby together, and it seemed that Elijah picked up on my agitated state. One nod toward Doctor Beiler, and the aging gentleman ushered everyone out of the room. I was grateful to have my family all to myself, and my husband was pleased with me. I felt the luckiest that a woman could ever be.

"I'm his mamma—his *mam*," I said proudly.

"And I'm his papa," Elijah said with a smile. "God has really blessed us."

Elijah bowed his head, and I knew that meant he wanted to pray. I bowed my head too, while cuddling my new baby at my breast.

ଞ୍ଚଓଷ

Three long days after Eli's birth, I was ready to get out of bed and walk with my new baby. I wanted to show him off to my best friend, who was so tired from her own pregnancy that she was unable to come to see me. Lucy, who was still staying with me, walked the short distance to Hannah's home with me. She didn't answer, however, when I knocked at the door, so we let ourselves in.

"Hello," I called loudly. "Hannah, are ya here?"

"In here," a weak voice called out to me.

We discovered her laying on the sofa in the front room, and she seemed awfully ill.

"Are ya sick?" Lucy asked Hannah.

"I'm in labor, but I couldn't get up to ring the dinner bell to get David's attention in the field," she managed after a long contraction.

"Lucy, go ring the bell, and tell David to come in just as soon as he comes up to the house," I ordered my sister.

I set my sleeping baby down on the floor after spreading out his blanket so I could assist my friend in getting to her feet. I knew she should be in her bed where it would be more comfortable. Getting her there was a difficult task due to the severity and closeness of her contractions. I knew this baby was not going to wait much longer to make its appearance, but I struggled with her in my still-weakened state. When I was finally able to get her comfortable in her bed, I went downstairs to get Eli so he wouldn't be out of my sight any longer.

Once inside Hannah's room, I could hear the familiar grunting sounds that I had made when I was pushing my baby into the world. I panicked at the thought of being the only one in attendance at this baby's birth, but I knew I had to appear calm for Hannah's sake.

"Jane, I'm afraid," she cried out.

"It's okay. I won't let anything happen to ya. Don't worry, I know just what to do," I assured her.

I said a quick prayer in my head to help get rid of my own fear.

Lord, give me strength to know what to do, and take away my fear. Protect Hannah and her baby from harm. And forgive me for lyin' to Hannah about knowin' what to do. Ya know I don't know, Lord, so bless me with wisdom so I'll know what to do.

Suddenly, Lucy entered the room and motioned for me to come out in the hall to speak to her.

"What is the problem?" I asked impatiently.

"I rang the bell seven times, and Mr. Yoder didn't come."

"Then run up and get Mamma to call Dr. Beiler. But ring that bell one more time on your way out," I ordered her.

"The doctor ain't gonna get here in time anyhow, so why should I run all that way?"

"Don't argue with me, girl," I warned her. "Do what I say. Hannah will need tendin' to after the birth and I can't do it. Now go!"

She didn't argue any further, but ran down the steps and out of the house. Just as I re-entered Hannah's bedroom, I heard the clang of the bell, and felt confident that it would bring David that time.

I need ya, Lord. Please don't leave me alone with Hannah.

"How're ya doin'?" I asked in a tone I thought reflected perfect composure.

"I think I can feel the baby coming," she said, wincing. "Will ya look and see for me, Jane."

"Don't ya wanna wait for the doc to get here?"

"Please, Jane. I would do it for you."

She was right. The baby's head began to emerge.

There was no time to think about it. With one small push, I caught her baby girl as she entered the world. We both laughed and cried a little as I laid the baby on her chest and wrapped the blanket around her. The baby began to scream, alerting David who had just entered the room. He quickly ran to his wife's side.

"I'm sorry I didn't get here in time." He smoothed Hannah's hair and kissed her gently on her cheek. "I was at the opposite end of the field with that ornery horse of mine, and couldn't get him to budge. Because of the hour, I thought it was time to come up for dinner, and I figured I could just be a little late. I'm so sorry, Hannah."

"It's all right. I know that horse has been giving you a tough time. Besides, I think Jane did a wonderful job."

She was beaming from ear to ear, and I blushed a little at her comments.

"Jane, you should be a midwife," she joked.

"No way! I was scared to death. Couldn't ya see that?"

"You were really calm for being so afraid. I knew the good Lord was watching over all three of us," she said cuddling her baby.

She adjusted the baby a little, and tried to hold her up toward her husband so he could get a better look.

"Meet your daughter, Rachel," she said to David.

"Hello, Miss Rachel," he said as he kissed his wife's cheek.

"Jane, I want to see your baby. In all the excitement, I forgot all about seeing him," she said apologetically.

I held up Eli so she could see him. The couple commented on his beauty before I bid them goodbye. As I was leaving, Doctor Beiler arrived.

"You're too late," I joked with him.

"I can see that. Did you do the delivering?"

"Yes, Sir."

"Well then ya ought to consider being a midwife. It looks as though ya did a mighty fine job here."

"No thanks. I think I'll stay away from pregnant women who are about to deliver from now on," I said, offering a final wave to the new family.

ඔ03

With the cool weather of October came the arrival of a baby girl named Autumn to Nadine and Benjamin. It wasn't a traditional Amish name, but everyone in the family liked it. They had the name Adam picked out if the baby had been a boy, but Nadine said they would save it for their next child, hoping for a boy. Nadine was happy that she had an easy labor, the same as I had with Eli.

ඔ03

Eli grew fast. So fast, in fact, that I had trouble keeping up with him. My mother said he was a quick learner. It seemed that everything he did, she claimed that he was early in his accomplishments. He didn't even crawl for more than a week. He was on the go, and could practically run before he had mastered his walking skills. Talking was another issue where the tot excelled. Elijah was so proud of his son's intelligence that he loved to show him off at family gatherings. At only fifteen months, Eli would talk on and on about farm-related topics with Elijah and the other adult men; things that even I didn't understand. In some ways, it seemed that my young son was more intelligent than I was; which made me feel a little intimidated.

As time went by, I spent a lot of time reading to him, and by the time he was a year and a half, he was repeating entire books to me from memory. He felt proud of himself that he was *reading* the book to me instead of having me read to him all the time. Elijah suggested we get him some new ones since he had become bored with reading the same ones repeatedly.

For his second birthday, Elijah and I picked out several books at the library sale in town. A few were children's chapter books, and I hoped they would keep his attention longer than the usual short story books that were designed for his age group. The simpler ones only seemed to bore him, and he longed for a more challenging story to be read to him.

Birthdays always meant a family gathering. There were now so many birthdays, that between spouses and grandchildren, it seemed we were getting together almost weekly for someone's birthday. At Eli's birthday party, he was so delighted with the baseball and bat from his grandparents that he wanted to skip the food and go straight out and play. Elijah allowed him to have his way, so my mother, Naomi, Rebekah and Nadine assisted me in moving the party out to the brick patio.

"You look a little pale, dear," Naomi commented to me.

"I think the heat of July is getting to me. I've been a bit tired the last few days."

"When was your last cycle, honey," she asked gently.

The question caught me off guard, and I felt uneasy discussing such a personal subject with Elijah's *mam*. Still, I answered her.

"Well, let's see. I think it was some time in May, and now we're in July...oh no!"

I sat down on one of the painted patio chairs and thought about the accuracy of my answer for a moment. I guess I'd been a little careless in keeping track of it, but to the best of my calculations, I had correctly stated the obvious. A smile came over my face as I remembered Elijah's reaction to the news of my pregnancy with Eli. He had swept me off my feet in his excitement. Before I could sort out my own feelings about it, *Mam*, Naomi, Rebekah and Nadine were hugging me excitedly.

Laughter arose from the crowd of men and boys that had joined in the game of baseball with Eli. With such a mixture of ages, it seemed a small miracle that they could carry on an actual game. When it was Eli's turn, Elijah picked him up and ran with him around their makeshift field so the two-year-old could score a run. Mitchell and his young son were on the same team with my father, along with my two younger brothers, Cameron and Sammy. Matthew Beiler and David Yoder joined Elijah, his papa, and Eli after leaving their wives with the rest of the women on the patio. Hannah and Deborah were delighted to share in my recent discovery.

"I was wondering when you were going to work on increasing your family. David and I are having another one too," Hannah confided. "From the sounds of things, we will be due about the same time again. I was planning on telling you when we got together for Rachel's second birthday in three days, but this turned out perfectly."

ഔരു

At Rachel's party, it was revealed that both Nadine and Rebekah were also expecting.

"Why didn't ya say anything the other day?" I asked them.

"Sometimes too much news at one time can be overwhelming," Rebekah offered.

Nadine agreed. I didn't, but I was excited anyway. It was going to be tough for all of us to be pregnant at the same time. One thing was for certain—it would probably slow us down some when we had our canning bee. Most things were ready to be harvested and canned, and with all of us pregnant and tired all the time, it would add to the burden that our own mothers would have in assisting us. It would be rough on our mothers having to do more than their share of work at the canning bee, but we knew they would be of any help they could during our time of confinement.

Word came to us later that week that Deborah and Matthew were expecting also, as were Elijah's cousin, Jonathon, who married Miriam Miller. The community around us was growing by leaps and bounds. I was grateful that our children would have plenty of cousins their own ages to play with at all the family dinners.

ଧ୬ଓଃ

Abigail arrived five weeks early. Although she looked frail at only four pounds, eleven ounces, Doctor Beiler gave Elijah and me the reassurance that all was well with her. He proved to be correct. She was a strong baby, and gained almost two pounds in the first four weeks.

Eli was happy to be a big brother, and loved to help me with the diaper changing duties. The newness soon wore off when he discovered he enjoyed milking the cows with his papa, rather than looking after a baby that didn't do much other than sleep and eat. Elijah had been letting him help with the chores since Abigail's birth, in an attempt to give me some quiet time with the new baby.

ଧ୬ଓଃ

By the time we reached Abigail's actual due date; she had gained nearly three pounds. Nadine, Rebekah and Hannah had their babies—all boys, within the week. Nadine and Benjamin decided they would name their son, Adam. Since they named their daughter, Autumn, they felt they would stay with names that began with the letter "A". I didn't question them, I figured they had their reasons, and it wasn't that important for me to pry.

Mitchell and Rebekah named their baby Ira, after my Uncle Ira. My father was pleased that his deceased brother's name would go on in the family. Hannah and David chose the name, Noah. I thought it suited the happy-go-lucky tot because he was so calm he appeared not to have a care in the world.

Abigail was easier to take care of than Eli had been. She slept most of the day and night. Often, I would have to wake her at feeding time, then, she would go back to sleep until it was feeding time again. This came in handy for my spring planting. I had worried over how I would manage with a new baby to tend to, but she slept under the umbrella near my garden for a good portion of the day. Occasionally, I would lie on the quilt next to her and watch her sleep when I was taking a break from my work. The gentle spring breeze and the constant song from nesting birds seemed to keep her in a lulled state.

ഇൗരു

"Eli's third birthday is comin' up," I said to Elijah over dinner.

"I can't believe how much he's grown," Elijah said. "He is getting mighty *gut* at milking the cow, *jah?*"

"He looks like a short version of his papa when he's hard at work," I said.

The young boy had turned out to have the same wispy blonde hair and sparkling blue eyes that Elijah had been blessed with. Abigail, on the other hand, favored me in her facial features, and her eyes were greenish-blue in color. She already had long locks of golden hair. She actually reminded me a lot of Lucy at that age.

"I would like to make the boy a train, with a track and a small city to go around it," Elijah continued our conversation.

"Ya only have three weeks. How in the world are ya gonna get it finished in time?"

"Most of the big work around the farm is finished for the time being, so I could work it in after chores," he said with determination in his voice.

"I know ya get everything done that ya set your mind to. I don't doubt that you'll have it done in time," I retracted.

"Would ya like to help me build the city, and paint the train?"

"I'd love to help ya with it!" I said excitedly.

ഇരുതു

For the next eighteen days, Elijah and I worked side by side in the barn preparing our son's present. It was nice to have so much time with my husband, a rarity that I had not had the pleasure of too much in our nearly four-year marriage. We had our picnics on our anniversary, but we had not spent several days in a row being together for most the day. It was nice having my mother, Nadine and Hannah take turns in caring for our two children so we could take the extra time to finish the project.

When Eli's birthday finally arrived, Elijah and I were proud of the job we had done in making our son such a big present. I had made him some new clothing too, but when he saw the train he was no longer interested in anything else. This made the grandparents a little leery of how the young boy would accept their gifts. My parents spoiled him with a tricycle, which he promptly begged to ride on the patio. So as not to insult his parents, Elijah made Eli sit still for Abraham's and Naomi's gift. They got him a small molded plastic yard pool from the hardware store in town. I was shocked at the gift, since they were not known to shop for gifts—they firmly believed in hand-crafted items. Eli whined until Elijah and Abraham agreed to fill it with water so he could splash in it after he rode his new trike.

ൟൟ

The following weeks were filled with harvesting and canning bees between the women in the small community. My sister, Rachel began courting Elijah's cousin, Daniel Zook. At fifteen, she was a year younger than I had been when I began to court Elijah. My husband didn't think it was a good idea, but I reminded him of how eager he and I had been when we wanted so badly to court before we were allowed. I figured that as lax as my father was getting on his courting rules, Molly might be only twelve when she got herself a beau. I tried to voice some concerns to my father, but he had a mind of his own and I could see it was made up.

As the months wore on, Rachel seemed more grown up, and she and I actually began to have a better relationship. She had even helped Nadine and me with the canning, which was not like her. Nadine and I both could see that Daniel was taking the rebel out of our little sister. I was personally glad to see her settle down and be more of a lady than the tomboy that she had been most of her life. My mother nearly worked over-time fashioning dresses that would replace Rachel's usual wardrobe of trousers and collared shirts. My father commented that it was nice to have his *daughter* back. He even joked with her that she could pass her old things on to Cameron or even to Sam when he was big enough to wear them. She didn't appreciate those types of remarks in Daniel's presence, but my father was never one for using manners in front of company.

ൟൟ

In the spring of 1985, I gave birth to our third child—a son, which we named Simon. He was a weak child, and Doctor Beiler spent more time at our home that first six days, than I had seen him in all the years I'd known him.

After he had survived his first week, I thought Simon seemed to be a bit stronger. One afternoon, after nursing him, he fell asleep in my arms; I held him and watched him sleep. Suddenly, he fell limp in my arms, his coloring appearing slightly bluish around his mouth and eyes. I jiggled him slightly, causing him to cough and spit up. My heart fluttered for a moment, and I wondered if he had stopped breathing. I held him most of the remainder of the day, and even watched him sleep much of that night. I didn't mention it to Elijah at the time, for I wasn't certain if it were uneventful, or if it was a life-threatening occurrence.

In the early hours of the morning, before even Elijah stirred, I sat in the wicker rocking chair out on the balcony that was off our bedroom. I nursed Simon, and held him, willing him to grow stronger. The sun began to peak over the clouds that had formed along the horizon, painting the sky with the most glorious, majestic hues. Sparrows were busy building a nest in the treetops that spread out close to the balcony. I strained my neck to watch them working without disturbing them. As I watched the birds and wondered what God had in store for my baby's life, I was reminded of some verses I read in my Bible in the book of Matthew.

Look at the birds of the air, they do not sow or reap or store away in barns, and yet your heavenly Father feeds them. Are you not much more valuable than they? Who of you by worrying can add a single hour to his life? Are not two sparrows sold for a penny? Yet not one of them will fall to the ground apart from the will of your Father. And even the very hairs on your head are all numbered. So don't be afraid; you are worth more than sparrows.

With the rising of the sun, came the promise of a new day, and I knew without a doubt that my baby's life rested in God's hands.

LITTLE WILD FLOWER

Book Two

Don't miss the continuing story of Jane and Elijah...just when Jane thought her life in the Amish community couldn't get any better, tragedy strikes the Zook farm. Jane is suddenly lost in the world she created with Elijah, and flees to her home town in search of the past she left behind so many years before. But coming face-to-face with the pain of her childhood sends her running back to the very community she now feels disconnected from. Struggling with the decision she made at the age of fifteen that changed the lives of her entire family, Jane must now determine if she can continue to live in the Amish community, or if she will try to salvage the past she still craves. What she discovers as she reunites with friends she left behind in her teen years will make her stronger, and bring joy to her life again...

Purchase Little Wild Flower: Book Two, to find out what happens next for Jane and Elijah.

Log onto FaceBook and search Livingston Hall Publishers for all the details.

Thank you for reading…

To my dear mother, Ann Marie...

If you're looking down from Heaven, I'm certain you're smiling. My only regret is that I was unable to finish reading this to you before you left this world...

Made in the USA
Lexington, KY
11 April 2012